A FLIGHT OF DRAGONS

A SHORT STORY COLLECTION

DEBBIE MUMFORD

WDM
Publishing

COPYRIGHT

was worth it. I hope Ms. Mumford writes more in this world. I love these characters."

～

Dragon Slayer from Amazon: Five stars: "I liked the characters and the story line. For those that love a mystery and a good romance along with the paranormal, this book is for you."

～

Praise for *Sorcha's Heart*

Katie from Goodreads: Five stars: 'This story was fantastic...I strongly recommend anyone who likes paranormal dragon stories read this. Best prequel ever. Off to look for more by this author."

～

Old Ozark Gal from Amazon: Five stars: "...for those who enjoy a sizzling relationship without the graphic descriptions of what body part goes where, this is an excellent book. So what are you waiting for? Go read it!"

～

Karyn-Anne from Amazon: Five stars: "The romantic scenes were full of passion and heat, but not graphic or explicit. I really, really enjoyed this novella ... Very highly recommended!"

～

Ahmari from Amazon: Five stars: "This book is very well written ... I liked it so much I purchased the sequel! ... a unique idea for a fantasy and told in a delightful manner. I look forward to reading more from this author."

～

Praise for *Her Highland Laird*:

Katharina from Amazon: Five stars: "I'm normally not someone who reads romance novels, but … I stumbled over Debbie Mumford's Romance stories. This one was an absolute treat. Not only did it depict the life in 15th century correctly (well researched for such a short story), it evokes emotion very well … I'll definitely read more by this author."

～

Tony from Amazon: Five stars: "Very interesting story. With some suspense and an interesting thread of love."

DEBBIE MUMFORD

BESTSELLING AUTHOR OF *SORCHA'S HEART*

The
White
Dragon
and the
Red

The floor of Edith's chamber was strewn with fresh, sweet-smelling rushes and a warm fire crackled on the hearth adding the scent of pine and a whiff of smoke to the air. Harold, her hand-fast husband of more than twenty years, sat before the fire wrapped in a soft woolen robe of royal purple. Edith had washed the battle grime from his limbs with her own hands, and now, as he leaned back in the sturdy wooden chair, she combed his long auburn hair.

Once his hair had shone like burnished copper, alive with golden lights, but now those lights had dimmed to pewter and the copper had faded and lost its sheen. Placing the carved wooden comb on a low side table, Edith dipped her fingers in a small silver bowl of mint-infused oil and began rubbing it into Harold's temples. She knew from long experience that the pressure and motion of her fingers combined with the soothing odor of the mint would ease a headache and help her lord find restful sleep.

How many times had she performed such ministrations for this man? After how many battles had she eased his pain and helped calm his mind? Too many to count, and yet, she treasured the memories, and the knowledge that she had been a good wife to this powerful man.

She had been so young when her father had given her in hand-fast marriage to the newly named Earl of East Anglia. Harold had been in his mid-twenties, tall and handsome and battle-tested. A warrior of renown. She hadn't been loath to marry, but neither had she known the man.

Fortunately, she had found joy in their union.

And now, twenty years and six healthy, well-grown children later, she still loved her husband... and knew that he cherished her as well.

But Harold was no longer simply an earl. He was now King of All England, and beset by many foes. He had need of all the support he could find, especially from the powerful church whose archbishop had placed the crown upon his head. The same church that refused to recognize Edith as his lawful wife, had instead named her harlot.

Harold had been forced by the Dead God's church to take another wife, the widow of the King of Wales. Edith knew that this new marriage was one of political convenience, but that knowledge did nothing to bank the fires of outrage that burned in her soul.

Twenty years.

Six fine children, including three sons.

But instead of being Harold's queen, she was known as his mistress. His whore.

Still, after his defeat of the Norwegian king, Harald Hardrada, at the Battle of Stamford Bridge, Harold had returned to her, his hand-fast wife, not his pretty little Welsh queen.

Edith would always be the one Harold turned to, no matter what the Dead God's church demanded.

2

Edith woke to find Harold already dressed in a belted chainmail top over a rust colored tunic, his leggings and boots wrapped securely in place with leather thongs. A warm woolen cloak, pointed metal helmet and a sturdy, round shield of leather-covered linden wood waited beside the door.

"My lord," she exclaimed, "where are you going? You've only just returned from battle. You should be resting still."

He turned to face her, his expression grim. "Aye. 'Twas what I expected as well, but though I've defeated one foreign claimant to my throne, another threatens our shores. William the Bastard's ships have been sighted off Pevensey Bay. I must march south."

Edith swallowed her fear and forced her voice to calm. "But my lord, what of your men? Your housecarls and thegns sustained heavy damage against the Norsemen. Can they fight again so soon?"

Harold strode to the bed, took her face in his hands, and kissed her gently on the lips.

"They must," he said. "We must drive William back to Normandy." And turning, he strode from the room.

Edith sat alone in the large bed as fear curled in her belly and an ominous *knowing* bloomed in her mind.

He would die.

Her husband, her lord, her king.

Harold would die.

Closing her eyes and steeling her will, she made her choice. He would *not* die. She would protect him, and she would align herself with his pretty little Welsh queen to ensure that he did not meet his death in the coming battle.

What would it matter which of them was acknowledged Queen of England if the Bastard killed their King?

Ealdgyth, daughter of Aelfgar, widow of Gruffydd ap Llywelyn, wife of King Harold II would join Edith in the battle for their husband's life… or Edith would know the reason why.

Edith dressed quickly in her favorite deep blue tunic and fastened a rose mantle about her shoulders. She left the hood down, but braided her long dark hair and fastened the curling tendrils that escaped away from her face with a slender silver circlet. Her hair might no longer shine as it did in her youth, but it was still thick and dark.

When she was ready, she wrapped herself in a warm, fleece lined cloak and left the bower she had shared with Harold in the castle set aside for his use in York. Moving quietly through the unfamiliar passageways, she found her way up a stone staircase to a chilly tower. Heaving open a heavy wooden door, she stepped out onto the encircling walkway and leaned against the cold stone parapet.

Closing her eyes and opening her mind, she called to the White Dragon, the protector of the Midlands where she had grown to young womanhood. Never before had she sought the dragon's intervention in her husband's battles, but never before had he been threatened by a foreign duke when his own forces were weakened and battle-weary.

Great Wyrm, Wyvern of the low hills and gentle valleys of my birth, hear me now.

Edith poured all the belief and supplication of her early training into her prayer. Her mother, Matilda, had been a wise woman and an initiate into the mysteries before she had been given in marriage to Edith's father. Matilda had taught her daughters well, and though Edith had never had cause to call upon the White Dragon before, she knew with a certainty beyond mere faith, that the Great Wyrm would hear her.

Sure enough, a voice pealed through her mind. A sending so powerful she was forced to her knees and had to press her hands against her ears. The sound was within, to be sure, but she needed the outside pressure to keep the balance within her skull and forestall the faint that edged her vision with darkness.

Edith, daughter of Matilda, I hear your call and recognize your right of birth to petition my aid. What would you ask?

Even when he stopped speaking, his voice echoed like an avalanche of stones against her tender mind. When she felt sufficiently recovered, she responded, though she feared their conversation might cause her death.

If she died in this supplication, so be it. Harold must live.

Inhaling deeply she framed her request and sent it winging to the great White Dragon.

Harold, King of All England and the father of my sons and daughters, is in grave danger. He rides south to Pevensey Bay to fight against William the Bastard, Duke of Normandy. I ask that you protect Harold, Great One, and the men he leads into battle.

A strange prickling invaded her mind. Not painful, but unexpected and foreign. She braced for the pain his next words would bring.

What are the battles of men to me, little one? I care not which humans crawl along the earth in my domain.

Edith breathed a sigh of relief. He had moderated his sending.

This time his voice soothed and warmed the edges of her mind, healing the hurts of his earlier message.

Her relief fled when his meaning registered.

But Great One, the Normans will not know you! They will not honor you as your deserve.

A soft, chiding sigh blew through her thoughts like a gentle breeze. *When have you honored me, daughter of Matilda? Have you thought of me even once since leaving your mother's domain?*

Shame overwhelmed her. The wyrm had the truth of it. What right did she have to ask his aid when she'd given him no thought, no honor, in the twenty years of her marriage. Only in her extreme need did she think of him now, and then only to seek his aid.

Forgive me, Great One.

A puff of solace touched her thoughts, followed quickly by a surge of ire.

You have betrayed me, daughter of Matilda, the dragon growled. *I see the shadow of another dragon in your mind. A great red beast with four legs as well as wings. Not a proper wyvern such as I!*

Edith shrank back against the stone parapet, her heart hammering in reaction to the dragon's clear wrath. What was he talking about? She'd had no thoughts of...

But she had. She had thought to seek Ealdgyth's aid in contacting the Red Dragon of Wales.

When her pulse rate slowed and she felt in control of herself again, she answered the White Dragon of the Midlands.

Nay, Great One. I know no other dragons, nor have I ever thought to seek congress with any save yourself. The red dragon you see in my thoughts belongs to Wales.

And what have you to do with Wales, little one?

Nothing, Great One, but my husband has another wife—do not ask me to explain, the ways of men are convoluted, especially where the Dead God's servants are concerned. This other wife was once married to the King of Wales, before he was killed in battle.

And what has that to do with me?

Edith closed her eyes and inhaled a deep, calming breath. *Since she and I are both bound to Harold, I hoped she might seek the aid of the Red Dragon of Wales.* She paused a moment before hurrying on, *Tell me, Great One, if she made this request, would you join Wales to protect England's king?*

A deep, rumbling grumble sounded in her mind and she made herself as small as possible as she huddled on the battlement. She had gone too far, suggesting that the mighty White Dragon might require the help of the Red Dragon of Wales. He would blast her mind to nothingness. Her children would find her crouched here, a drooling, helpless lump of flesh that had once housed their mother.

A shadow fell across Edith, and she opened her eyes to see a white dragon hanging suspended in the sky just beyond the parapet.

Come, little one. If you are so desperate for your lord's life that you would seek the aid of the woman who has supplanted you, I can hardly fail to grant your petition. Climb onto my back. I will carry you to your sister-wife.

Relief surged through Edith's heart and hope blossomed. Ealdgyth could hardly deny her if she arrived on the wings of a dragon!

4

Edith sat astride the White Dragon of the Midlands, secure in her position between two pointed spines taller than her seated height. Her booted feet were tucked beneath the dragon's wing joints, and she was very glad of her fleece lined cloak. She hadn't thought to wear gloves when she'd left York a-dragonback, but Ealdgyth had gifted her a fine, fur-lined leather pair before the two women left the castle in London.

She glanced to the west across the early October sky to see her sister-wife firmly settled between the neck ridges of a great red dragon. Wales had not failed to answer Ealdgyth's call. If the White Dragon would fight for Harold and England, then the Red would not be left behind.

The two dragons and their riders circled the skies above Hastings, observing the battle that raged below. The dragons had promised Edith and Ealdgyth they would defend Harold and his men, but only in extreme need. If men could win the battle on their own, they should do so.

From high above, Edith watched as her husband commanded his men. His army had marched more than 240 miles to intercept William's forces on the Sussex coast. Nearly 7,000 Normans stood against the weary Englishmen, but Harold's men stood firm behind hastily erected earthworks and prepared to employ their well-practiced shield wall, unaware that supernatural aid circled in the sky above their heads.

The armies were well matched, despite the forced march Harold's troops had endured, and the battle raged from early morning until well into the evening. The White and Red dragons withheld their aid until William's forces feigned flight, causing Harold's shield wall to break formation. When the Norman's turned and loosed a hail of arrows against the English, the dragons joined the fray.

They swept the arrows from the sky before buffeting the combatants with the wind from their wings, leaving none on their feet, on either side of the battle. Landing between the armies with a great bellowing roar, the Red Dragon of Wales scorched a line of fire into the land before William's men, while the White Dragon of the Midlands hung in the sky above the red's head.

As agreed in advance, the White Dragon spoke, and his words echoed across the field causing all men to cower.

"Invaders from across the sea," he boomed, "leave this land. The throne of England is for those who have grown here and love this land. It is not for the likes of you. Be gone from our shores."

"Be gone!" echoed the Red Dragon with growling menace.

William's men dropped their weapons and scattered, too anxious to find their ships to worry about carrying swords or spears.

The White Dragon turned to Harold's army. "Fear not, the White Dragon of the Midlands and the Red Dragon of Wales have come to ensure King Harold's victory. Return to your homes and live in peace, knowing that should the need arise, we will fly to your aid once more."

"But only if we are given proper honor," added the Red

Dragon. "And only if called upon by those who hold the right by blood."

The two dragons cleared a space on the battlefield and deposited their riders gently on the blood-soaked ground. Before departing, they allowed each woman to place a hand on their heads and bestowed a benediction on the sister-wives.

When the dragons were mere specks in the sky, Harold stepped forward to stand before his wives. "How is this possible?" he asked as his men milled around gathering their belongings and slapping each other on their backs. "How came you to bring dragons to the battle?"

Ealdgyth smiled and, placing a hand on his cheek, kissed him gently. "Ask Edith, your first wife." Then she turned to Edith and curtsied. "The Dead God's priests do not rule me, sister-wife. I am honored to be second to you in Harold's household. If it pleases our lord, bring your children and join our household in London. I would learn from you, Edith the Fair."

Edith inclined her head and responded solemnly. "Thank you, Queen Ealdgyth. I will discuss our future and our lodging with our lord and king." Turning to Harold, she threw her arms about his neck and whispered, "You are safe!"

Harold kissed her soundly, then stepped back and said, "Come, Edith. Tell me the tale of how you and Ealdgyth brought the White Dragon and the Red to the Battle of Hastings."

"Gladly," she said, taking his hand, content to *know* that she and Ealdgyth and the Great Dragons had changed the course of English history.

DEBBIE MUMFORD

Egg Thief

SPUN YARNS
A Thrilling Short Story

EGG THIEF

A mixture of terror and elation spur me down the steep, rocky slope. The harsh, cold wind buffets me, making it had to keep my leather-booted feet beneath me.

I can't slow down. Can't fall. If I so much as pause...she might come back, might realize what I've done. If she catches me on this unprotected slope, she'll roast me alive.

The backpack bounces against my shoulders, its warm, reassuring weight throwing off my balance. I've done it! I slipped into her lair, stole an egg, and made it back to the cold, fresh air of the mountainside.

I've got to keep moving, got to make it to the forest. She won't be able to find me once I reach the trees' thick canopy.

I pant, cold air numbing nose and cheeks and making my lungs ache. But the precious egg in my pack, the one I risked everything to steal, is safe and warm, protected by a nest of soft woolen blankets.

The ground beneath my feet levels, turning from rock to coarse, low grass and sedge. Tree line is within sight, its stunted larch and fir trees twisted by the constant fierce, cold wind that whistles past my ears and makes my eyes water.

I'm going to make it. Those scraggly trees aren't much, but they're my only hope. The first cover on this wind-swept mountainside. Just a little way beyond the tree line, the proper forest begins. Tall spruce, firs, and aspen with sufficient canopy to shield a fleeing man from even a dragon's sharp vision.

The worst is behind me. Once I gain the forest, I'll be safe.

Terror loosens its grip on my heart and exultation bubbles through my core. A near-hysterical giggle forces its way past my chapped lips. Truly, I've done it. The jade-green egg with dark blue mottling is mine. A prize beyond measure. And not just because of the gold I will demand. My reputation will be made once I return to the city with a dragon egg in my pack.

I savor the fruits of my stealth. All that remains is to reach the safety of the forest.

A shadow passes overhead, and I stumble, my foot snagging on a tangled mass of sedge. I catch my balance and glance up at the clear blue, cloudless sky. My breath seizes and my heart plummets.

A dragon wheels in the sky.

She has returned, recognized her loss, and hunted me.

My pulse thunders, beating twice its normal tattoo. Blood sings in my veins, throbs at my temples, tingles in my fingertips. A burst of energy propels me down the slope. I must reach those trees.

With a screech of indignation, the dragon plummets to earth, landing between me and the trees. The backwash from her wings knocks me off my feet. I twist as I fall, keeping the packed egg safe, but sustaining a nasty jolt to my shoulder and wrenching a knee.

I gain my feet and crouch, ready to run, but where?

The dragon, a solid mass of muscle and anger, easily as big as my two-room hut, unfurls her wings and hisses. Her long, snake-like tongue lashes the air between us.

Dragon stink fills my nostrils, a noxious mix of sulfur,

rotting meat and blood that solidifies the terror freezing my heart and paralyzing my thoughts. Pain throbs in shoulder and knee, darkening the edges of my vision. Bitter, poisonous bile gags me.

All is lost.

No way forward. Not past a hulking beast whose wings blot out the scraggly trees beyond.

No way back. Not across a barren slope of alpine tundra.

Death stares at me with malignant satisfaction.

The inevitability of my demise calms me, thawing my terror and freeing my mind. I still have a card to play. I still hold the egg.

She can't crush me for fear of harming the egg. Nor can she use flame against me.

While I hold her egg, we are at an impasse. I stare into her yellow, cat-slit eyes and know that she understands our stalemate as well.

I hunker down to think while the dragon studies me with narrowed eyes. She furls her wings and settles, the barbed tip of her tail tapping restlessly.

The elation of a few moments before has shriveled. I wish wholeheartedly I'd never imagined this foolhardy scheme. Why did I gamble my life on the insane possibility of stealing a dragon's egg?

For unimaginable wealth and everlasting glory.

To be the first man to climb the dragon's mountain and return with an unblemished egg.

To be the man who made it possible for the High King to take his place among the gods. To provide the key ingredient to the fabled elixir of immortality: the heart of an unborn dragon.

And all I have to do to make those dreams a reality is steal past a massive, angry dragon and make my way back to the city with my prize.

Before any scrap of a plan can present itself to my fevered

mind, the dragon's tail ceases its tapping and a soft, low coo swirls upon the wind.

I frown. Do dragons coo?

The coo sounds again, soft, melodious, remarkably like the call of a mourning dove. The dragon closes her eyes and lowers her head.

Is this my moment? Can I steal past her while she's not looking? Could I reach the cover of the trees?

I lean forward, gathering my legs beneath me, ready to spring.

The egg in my pack jumps, pulling against the straps on my shoulders, ruining my balance. I stumble forward a step or two, catch myself and scramble back, away from the dragon's cruel talons.

Sweat beads my forehead and drips down my nose. The egg jumps again, hard enough to pull me onto my rump.

The dragon waits quietly, eyes closed, cooing, the sound oddly welcoming.

Another jump nearly unseats me.

I wriggle out of the pack, pull it into my lap, and swipe my shirtsleeve across my sweaty brow. Opening the pack, I shove layers of soft wool aside to expose the precious egg. A crack mars its perfection.

My heart sinks. I've waited too long. The egg is hatching.

Even if I survive the dragon, there will be no elixir of immortality. Not without the heart of an unborn dragon.

A louder coo burbles from the mother dragon. I glance up. Her eyes remain closed, her wings furled. If I didn't know better, I'd think she was asleep.

On a gut level, I understand: she is focused on the hatching egg.

Now is my moment. I must leave the pack with its now useless egg and run for cover. She won't follow. She's not interested in me. All she wants is to see her offspring safely hatched.

I glance back up the mountain. Are the other eggs hatching?

Could I leave this one and grab another? If I did, would I be able to get it down the mountain before it hatched?

Slowly, carefully, I slide back from the nested egg.

The dragon ignores me, continuing to coo.

I stand, paralyzed with indecision. Escape past the dragon and return to the city, empty-handed, but alive, or seize this opportunity to return to the lair, grab another egg, and escape down a different path while she is focused on this hatchling's birth?

The voice of caution, my mother's voice, screams at me to run for the trees. To save myself. To live to scheme another day.

But another voice, a more daring voice speaks more convincingly. *When will you ever have such a chance again? You know where the dragon is and she doesn't care about you. A little peril could earn you riches and eternal glory. Seize the moment, or spend the rest of your life regretting its loss.*

I take a few cautious steps upslope, half expecting the dragon to pounce on me. She doesn't even open an eye. My injured knee aches, but does not give way. I turn and race full tilt back to the dragon's lair.

A few minutes later I step out of the howling wind, into the shelter of the cave. Leaning against cold rock, I stand on my good leg, resting my aching knee, and wait for my labored breathing to ease, for my eyes to become accustomed to the dark.

The air is fetid with dragon stink, the floor littered with broken bones and bits of moldering pelts, remnants of long-forgotten meals.

I push myself upright and limp into the gloom. At the rear of the cavern, the eggs huddle in a nest of stout limbs lined with the pelts of bears and wolves. Climbing into the nest was easier last time. Now my shoulder throbs with every heartbeat and my leg trembles with the strain of my injured knee. But I make it.

Exhausted, I collapse onto the warm, coarse furs and crawl to the mound of eggs. I only need one. One egg and fame and fortune will be mine.

I reach toward the mound of deeper darkness that is the pile of eggs, and encounter not a smooth, hard shell, but soft, leathery skin.

Disappointment floods my soul and I jerk my hand back. At least one of the eggs has hatched, but perhaps there is still hope. Perhaps a late bloomer languishes beneath its more advanced siblings.

I inch sideways and reach into the pile again.

Immediately glowing eyes pop open and soft, gurgling cries sound. Small bodies scurry in the dark, accompanied by snaps and cracks as shells are trodden upon. I soon find myself surrounded by blinking, luminous eyes.

By their pale light I see that all the eggs have hatched. Nothing remains on the furs but infant dragons and splintered shells.

My whole enterprise has been too late. I never had a chance of getting an unblemished egg back to the city.

My hopes dashed, I crawl back across the pelts. I still have to climb out of the nest and escape this accursed mountain. The task seems insurmountable now that no reward awaits me.

Disappointment makes me stupid. I've forgotten I'm in a dragon's lair. Forgotten that despite their small size, I am surrounded by dragons.

I am reminded forcibly when a hatchling bites into the calf of my injured leg and tears away both fabric and meat. I scream in agony, kick out with my good leg, my leather boot connecting firmly with a small body.

But it is too late. Blood pumps from my wound, exciting the hatchlings, turning their newborn hunger into a feeding frenzy.

I curl into a tight ball, hoping to protect my tender belly from sharp talons and teeth. My last sight before my vision darkens is of the mother dragon's arrival, bearing her final hatchling to the feast.

Her triumphant roar deafens me, and as oblivion descends, I think, *Mother was right. I should have run for my life...*

DEBBIE MUMFORD

BESTSELLING AUTHOR OF *SORCHA'S HEART*

God-Touched

A Thrilling Short Fantasy Tale

1

My fingernails were broken, my fingertips bleeding from scrabbling against rock as I climbed the cliff. If I could just make it to the top before the guards caught me and dragged me back to the temple, I might have a chance!

I'd been chosen by The Crone of the Gods to be a sacrificial lamb. It was an honor I didn't want and would deny with the last breath in my body.

While our whole Oasis celebrated my impending death, I ran for my life. I might be the Chosen of the Gods, but I had no intention of dying at seventeen.

I'd always known I was different. The Matriarch of our Oasis singled me out as God-Touched before my fifth birthday. My mother accepted the decree to present me to The Crone of the Gods on my natal day with quiet dignity, as was expected of a mother of our tribe. If it broke her heart to give me up, I never knew it.

I only knew that on my fifth birthday I was bathed by my favorite aunt, dried and perfumed by my eldest sister, and dressed in my finest garb by my grandmother, before being turned over to my mother who combed and braided my hair with gentle fingers. The women of my mother's tent stood silently as I was led from their midst, never to return. At least, never again to take shelter among them or play with their daughters. I would still make my home at the Oasis of my foremothers, but I would now belong to The Crone and, if my service was deemed acceptable, eventually to the Gods themselves. My mother's tent was honored to have produced one such as me.

They were even more honored when they realized I was to be sacrificed, that my blood was destined to protect our tribe.

I had other ideas, and so I began my desperate ascent of the cliff face that sheltered our temple.

Carved into the living rock of the cliffs, the temple was unlike the tents of our people. Permanent and unmovable, its entrance was decorated with graven images of animals that could not exist and shaded by ancient palm trees. Wide shallow steps led to the doorway that none but those chosen by the Crone could pass.

I'd spent the last twelve years within those stone walls, serving the Gods... and the Crone. But no more. Now I was climbing the cliff face above the temple's walls. Climbing to outrun my fate.

My hands bled and ached while my sandaled feet sought purchase on a rocky outcropping. I had to reach the top! Had to know if the shadow I had seen in my dreams was real.

The Gods existed. They whispered in my mind, telling me of cool sandstone walls and a large graceful cavern. Of embedded quartz crystals that glittered in the light of a magical sun. Of the gods themselves—huge beings who roamed the night sky on silent wings.

And because I'd confided these tales to the Crone, she'd decreed my death as a necessary sacrifice.

Men's voices called to me from far below. "Sarai! Come down! You'll fall to your death!" The temple guards. What did they care if I fell? The Crone had already proclaimed my death.

But she wanted it on her terms, not mine. She wanted to

plunge the knife into my chest and carve out my heart, not see my blood splattered uselessly on the sand of the Oasis.

I kept climbing. My breath coming in shallow gasps as I pulled my weight from one outcropping rock to the next. I reached a shallow ledge and perched there for a moment, catching my breath and wrapping my bleeding fingers in the hem of my dusty, white tunic dress. I'd pulled the hem between my legs and tucked it into my belt to keep the trailing length out of my way during my escape. Now I released the fabric to bind my hands.

Glancing up, I judged the remaining distance I needed to scale. Bandaged hands would make climbing more difficult, but my blood had slickened the rocks, making the last portion of my climb treacherous. Which endangered me more? Wrapped hands or blood-slick fingers?

The guards had given up their attempt to cajole me into coming down. Four were now climbing while six others jogged around the end of the cliff. They would follow the switchback trail that scaled the butte from the far side. A longer, but much safer route than the one I had chosen.

My heart plummeted. If I made it to the top, I'd have little time. Could I do it? Could I reach out to the Gods?

I'd always been content to listen to their speech, never attempting to speak to them in return. They spoke to me, but did that mean they were aware of me? Or was my ability to hear them simply a fluke of my bloodline?

I had no way of knowing.

And yet, in my desperation, I knew I had to try to call them. And I knew instinctively it must be done from the heights.

And so, I climbed.

Steeling my resolve, I re-tucked the remaining hem of my gown, flexed my bandaged hands, and began the last section of my climb to the top of the cliff.

2

I dragged myself over the edge of the cliff and collapsed in the scraggly grass that grew atop the butte.

How had I come to this?

I remembered the day my family had given me to the Crone...

Mother had dragged me to my knees, while she and Grand-mother prostrated themselves in the warm sand before the temple. I remained upright, staring at the wide shallow steps leading to a doorway that gaped black and deep, like a dreadful hunting cat waiting to swallow me whole. When The Crone appeared, I watched her with open curiosity. The Holy One was swathed from head to foot in white robes, richly embroidered with silver and gold thread. Even her eyes were hidden from my sight, though I had no doubt she saw me clearly. She glided down the steps and stopped before me so that I had to crane my neck to continue my study of the place where her face should have been. She ignored my brazen stare and spoke to my elders.

"Blessings on your tent, Basira," she said to my grandmother, "and upon your womb, Maram. May it quicken soon to replace this daughter you have sacrificed to the Gods." Neither woman replied, but remained still as the stone of the temple.

Though I couldn't see her eyes, I felt The Crone's gaze rest upon me. When she held out her hand, I rose without prodding and placed my hand in hers. The skin beneath the rings and fine chains of her rank was smooth and firm, her palms soft and well-oiled. She turned with no further word and led me up the steps and into the maw of the stone giant.

I did not look back.

But today I did.

I crawled to the edge of the cliff and looked over. Three of the guards were no more adept at rock climbing than I. Only one was making good headway. He was already nearly halfway to the top.

My time of rest and reflection was at an end. If I was going to call the Gods, I had to do it now, before the guard could reach me and overpower me. Once I was back in the Crone's hands my life would end quickly. She would not delay even for a more auspicious moment. I would not be given another chance to escape.

I strode well away from the edge, but staying far from the mouth of the switchback trail. Bracing myself, I straightened my spine and stood as tall as my short stature allowed. I closed my eyes and breathed deeply, inhaling the scents of sage and sand, exhaling worry and fear. When I felt sufficiently calm and centered, I concentrated on the voices whispering in the back of my mind. A glowing thread appeared in my mind's eye. I touched it… and my world expanded.

3

The voices quieted. They didn't disappear. I could still feel their presence, but their chatter ceased. An air of expectation consumed my thoughts.

At last, a single deep voice spoke.

"Who are you? Your mind is not like ours."

I gasped and fell to the rocky ground, but held tightly to the glowing thread in my mind.

"I am Sarai. Are you a god?"

Warmth lit my soul with a quiet laugh.

"We are not gods, though we may seem so to you. What are you?"

I scooted around and sat cross-legged where I'd fallen, folding my bandaged hands in my lap.

"I am Sarai, a young woman of the Oasis."

"Ah," said the voice, its tones smooth and soothing. "You are human."

"Yes," I said, nodding though the voice could not see me. "If you are not a god, what are you?"

"We are dragons of the Desert Weyr."

Dragons! I was talking to a dragon!

A sound caught my attention and I opened my eyes. The temple guard was pulling himself onto the rocky surface of the plateau where I sat.

Fear spiked through my blood.

"What is wrong, Sarai?" the dragon asked. "I feel your fear."

"My death approaches," I cried aloud.

The guard stopped and stared at me, his grizzled face quizzical. "I mean you no harm, Sarai. You are the Chosen of the Gods. I would not dare to harm you."

The voice in my head spoke again, and I closed my eyes, concentrating on his words.

"Where are you, Sarai? I will come to you."

I thought of my location, careful not to say the words aloud. The temple guard now stood beside me, but he'd made no move to touch me.

"We come," said the dragon.

4

Before the dragon could arrive my whole tribe joined me on the plateau atop the cliffs.

The temple guards had all found their way to the top, both those who scaled the rocky wall and those who trod the switch-back trail. None had been willing to touch me. I was the Chosen of the Gods, and as long as I sat quietly on the ground with my eyes closed, they did not dare interrupt my meditations.

I had no intention of giving them a reason to drag me back to the temple.

After conferring among themselves, one was chosen to return to the Oasis and ask the Crone what was to be done.

She had evidently decided that my sacrifice could take place on the heights as easily as on the temple's wide steps. And so she made the announcement: the entire tribe was to gather on the plateau to observe the rite.

I hadn't escaped. I'd simply changed the venue for my death.

My people surrounded me. They'd appeared from the switch-back trail in twos and threes and family groups. The Crone had arrived in a litter lined with soft pillows and carried by even more temple guards.

The stage was set for my death. The ceremonial knife, its gold hilt shining in the sun, rested on a pure white prayer rug decorated with silver and gold threads. The Crone only waited for the most auspicious moment: dusk. When the sun dipped behind the horizon, flooding the sky with blood red color, my blood would stain the rocky soil of the plateau.

I was doomed.

Unless the dragon arrived before dusk.

Were the dragons even real? Or had I imagined the voices in my mind? Perhaps I was delusional. If so, I would soon be dead.

As the afternoon wore on the plateau became littered with temporary shelters, sun shades erected for the comfort of my tribe. As soon as her lavish pavilion was complete, the Crone sent for me. My face and hands were washed with scented water, my hair combed and oiled, and my damaged hands properly attended to.

I didn't understand why they bothered when my death was imminent.

With the ceremonial knife gleaming beside her, the Crone, dismissing her attendants, called me to sit with her. She poured a cup of cool tea for me with her own hands, and urged me to refresh myself.

"You know," she said, "I hold you in no disfavor, Sarai. I'm sorry to be the instrument of your death."

"Then why single me out?" I asked, sipping the sweetened tea. "Our people rarely perform human sacrifices. Why me?"

A small frown creased her forehead. "I think you know why, and it is too bad. You're a bright young woman. I'd hoped you would become Crone when my time is done. But alas, you disqualified yourself from that possibility."

"Because I confided in you that I hear voices," I said, and took another sip.

She nodded. "Yes. We knew you were God-Touched as a child, but thought you'd outgrown the affliction." She shrugged and picked up her own tea cup. "Unfortunately, we were wrong. You were simply much better at hiding the effects than the others."

"Others?" My pulse pounded behind my ears. I wasn't the only one? There had been others who heard the voices? Why did I not know this? Where were they?

She glanced at me, eyes widening in surprise. "You did not know? We always assumed the voices explained such things to those like you."

"What happened to the others?" I asked. "Why have I not met them?"

Her laughter danced through the pavilion, floating out into the heat of the summer afternoon. "Where are they? Why they are dead, of course! Every Crone is warned in her turn, if a God-Touched reaches maturity with the affliction intact, she must be sacrificed. You are the first to be found in a generation."

I stilled, the cup hovering near my lips. Despair stole my thirst. There had been others like me and they had all died. The dragons, gods or not, had not saved them. Not a single one.

I'd been a fool to believe in dragons. The Crone was right. The voices were an affliction. A disease that couldn't be allowed to spread through our community. I wasn't God-Touched. I was insane.

I set my cup aside and buried my face in my damaged hands. There was no escape. I would die... for the good of the community.

Comforting hands patted my shoulder. "Do not mourn, Sarai," the Crone said, her voice soothing and kind. "You will be remembered as a holy woman, not as a disease carrier. That is our gift to you and your mother's tent."

Small comfort to one who wished only to live.

The glowing thread in my mind sparked to life. "We come," the deep voice said. "Prepare yourself."

I scrambled to my feet and raced from the Crone's pavilion to stand alone at the edge of the temporary sun shades. One hand shaded my eyes as I searched the skies, the other covered my mouth to hold back the cry of hope I longed to release.

The Crone hurried to my side. She stopped and studied me with narrowed eyes. "What are you doing?" she asked. "What is happening?"

I removed my hand from my lips and pointed at the sky. As if released by my movement, a hysterical giggle bubbled up from my core and spilled across the plateau. A wing of five dragons were clearly visible in the afternoon sky. Blue. Brown. Green. Red. And one of deep purple. Their scales shone in the afternoon sun.

"What have you done?" the Crone cried, backing away from me.

Indeed, all of my people scattered. They cowered in under their sun shades, hid behind rocks, or rushed down the switch-back trail. Anything to get away from the center of the plateau where I now stood alone.

Alone. As I had always been, whether I understood it or not.

And unafraid.

These dragons would not hurt me. They had not come to kill me, but to rescue me from my people. My people who intended to cut out my heart to save themselves from contagion at my hands.

Who then were my people? The dragons who sought to know me, or the humans who sought to kill me?

"You are Sarai," the deep voice proclaimed as the purple dragon landed before me.

"I am," I agreed, and without considering the consequences ran to him and threw my arms as far around his neck as I could reach. "Thank you for coming!"

All five dragons, the one who sheltered me beneath his wing and the four who hovered in the sky, threw back their heads and roared their delight. And in my mind, I heard the echoes of cele-bration from the many dragons who had remained behind in the

Desert Weyr. They rejoiced to find me safe and whole. But mostly they rejoiced to find me. To know I existed.

For reasons I did not understand, the weyr considered me their own, the jewel of their future!

I had found my people… and they wore scales and traveled on the wind.

Eventually I would mourn for those God-Touched who died before they could find their tribe, but right now I rejoiced!

"Tell them," my scaly purple protector growled, "tell them that if they kill another of our people, we will destroy them in a fiery inferno. None will survive."

I glanced up into his eye, high above my head, and nodded.

Stepping from the shelter of my protector's wings, I called to my former tribe, "People of the Oasis, hear me!" I pointed at the Crone where she cowered among the pillows of her pavilion. "The Crones have known for generations that some born among you were different. God-Touched, they called us. Know now that the dragons of the Desert Weyr claim us as kin."

I walked to the Crone and, offering her my hand, pulled her to standing.

"Neither the dragons nor I will hold you responsible for past actions, but the weyr has decreed, if another God-Touched is sacrificed, they will destroy the Oasis and all who live there. Do you understand?"

The Crone nodded, her eyes downcast, but that wasn't good enough. I needed—no, the weyr needed—to hear the words.

"Speak," I commanded.

She raised her chin and met my gaze. "I understand. I will set the command in stone. All future Crones will know that the God-Touched are under the protection of the Desert Weyr."

I smiled at the roar of acceptance that sounded in my mind.

"When a God-Touched comes of age," I said, inspiration striking, "tell them to climb to this plateau and reach out to the voices only they can hear. We will be waiting."

"We will be waiting," agreed my purple-scaled protector's voice. "Come, Sarai. The weyr waits to greet you."

I bowed to the Crone before turning and running to my purple-scaled friend. He held out his front leg and planted a picture in my mind of how to climb onto his back for flight. Scaling a dragon and settling between his neck ridges was not nearly as difficult as climbing the cliffs to the plateau... and it didn't even cause my hands to bleed.

"You have bled enough, Little Sister," he murmured in my mind. "No more."

His muscles bunched beneath me and with a powerful leap, we joined the others in the air.

I was flying! On a dragon! On my way to meet my kin and begin a new life.

Perhaps I had been sacrificed after all. I had shed my blood for my people, be they human or dragon, and left all that I had known behind.

I was truly God-Touched.

Uncollected Anthology

WERE-CREATURES & CONUNDRUMS

ISSUE 33 UA APRIL 2024

DISAPPEARED!

DEBBIE MUMFORD

1

I raced down the hill from my apartment on Highland Road to the main campus of the State University of New York at Geneseo. Even this early in the morning the air was warm; the day would be a hot one. How could the air be sweet with the fragrance of summer flowers? How could the blue sky sport fluffy white clouds? My life was falling apart. The sky should be dark and weeping buckets of rain in sympathy for my loss!

Just a few more blocks. I'd almost made it to campus, thank heavens! My dark brown hair was pulling loose from my ponytail and my bell-bottom jeans and peasant blouse were damp with sweat. But Bailey Hall was one of the first buildings I'd encounter on this trajectory. My race was almost over.

Dr. Godwin had to be in his office. I had to talk to him. Now!

Surely the police would listen to a tenured anthropology professor. They'd ignored me, but they wouldn't ignore Dr. Godwin!

I sucked in a labored breath and struggled not to sob. Running was more important than crying. Crying wouldn't help; Dr. Godwin would.

But it was hard not to cry when Bruce was gone!

Vanished.

Disappeared.

His phone simply rang and rang until his answering machine picked up. I'd left several increasingly frantic messages, but he hadn't returned my call.

His apartment was empty, his bed unslept in. I knew this because, as his fiancé, I had a key.

When I couldn't find him, I'd gone straight to the police. The officer I spoke with was very kind, even sympathetic, but refused to do anything. College students went on benders all the time. Bruce would surface when he sobered up. Maybe he'd run off with friends to Rochester for a night on the town. The city was only 35 miles north of campus. Even Buffalo, just over an hour's drive from Geneseo, wasn't out of the question.

No, the police weren't concerned. Bruce wasn't missing. He was just playing hooky from his summer classes, simply blowing off a little steam.

But they didn't know Bruce. I did.

Bruce didn't drink and he didn't go to clubs. He was the most responsible guy I'd ever met. An anthropology graduate student, Bruce was Dr. Godwin's teaching assistant. He took his duties very seriously. He wouldn't disappear and leave Dr. Godwin in a lurch.

And Bruce was engaged. To me. He wouldn't just run off to Rochester or Buffalo or anywhere else without telling me. If he left Geneseo, he'd take me with him!

My lungs burned as I ran past the sub shop where Bruce and I frequently ate lunch. The smell of freshly baked bread filled the air, but I couldn't enjoy the aroma. I needed my breath to finish my race to campus.

Almost there. Bailey Hall was in sight. Dr. Godwin *had* to be in his office. He was the only one who would take me seriously. He knew Bruce. He'd understand. Dr. Godwin would know what to do.

Not taking the time to run around the building to the main entrance that faced the quad, I flung the back door of Bailey Hall open and ran into the deserted main floor corridor. Not a lot of students stuck around for summer session, so classes were small and often held outdoors or scheduled later in the day. My footsteps echoed along the linoleum floors as I headed to Dr. Godwin's office.

He had to be there. He just had to!

Reaching his office door, I paused to catch my breath, tucking stray wisps of hair behind my ears. Forcing myself to at least appear calm, I knocked, holding my breath and praying he'd answer.

"Come," a male voice called from beyond the door. I breathed a sigh of relief.

Opening the door, I peered around its edge. "Do you have a moment, Dr. Godwin? I need your help."

Drake Godwin sat behind a massive dark wood desk. Matching floor-to-ceiling bookshelves lined the walls behind and to his right. To his left, a good-sized window looked out on campus. He glanced up from one of the many papers that littered the surface of his desk, his expression quizzical.

I'd met Dr. Godwin at a cookout he'd hosted for his students at his cabin on Conesus Lake. I wasn't invited, but Bruce was and my fiancé had taken me along as his guest. Then, as now, I was surprised by the professor's dark good looks. His complexion spoke of days in the summer sun, though Bruce swore the man rarely left Bailey Hall. Godwin's hair and eyebrows were so black they shone with blue highlights. His eyes, though not as dark as his hair, seemed more black than brown, and his features gave new meaning to the word chiseled.

He was a devastatingly handsome man, with the sleeves of his white button-down shirt rolled up and his green plaid necktie precisely knotted, but his arrogance and haughty demeanor held people, especially female students, at a distance. Dr. Godwin was a formidable man.

"You're not one of my students," he said in a dismissive tone. "Are you sure you've come to the correct office?"

I thought of Bruce and swallowed the impulse to cower. Stepping fully into the room, I nodded. "My name is Lucy Winters, I'm engaged to Bruce James. Your TA."

His quizzical expression morphed into an annoyed frown. "I know who my teaching assistant is, young lady. As you can see, Bruce isn't here. Go look for him elsewhere. You're interrupting my research." Having dismissed me, he returned to the document he'd been reading when I came in.

"But that's just it, Dr. Godwin," I cried, desperate to regain his attention. "He's not anywhere! He's disappeared. I've searched everywhere; he's nowhere to be found."

"Don't be dramatic," he scoffed. "He probably stepped out for coffee."

His attitude drowned my panic and ignited my anger. "Excuse me," I said, my voice little more than a snarl. "I expected that attitude from the police, but I thought you cared about him. I expected you to help me, not scold me like some teenage girl with her first crush. Bruce is missing and no one but me seems to care."

Godwin frowned again, but this time the annoyance didn't seem to be aimed at me. He cocked his head, studied me for a moment, then rose from his chair and walked around his desk.

Gesturing me toward the door, he said, "If you'll just wait in the hall, I'll make a some enquiries."

"I'd rather stay."

"I'd rather you didn't." So saying, he stepped past me, opened the door, and nodded me out.

"Fine," I said, "but I'm not going anywhere."

"I expected nothing less," he said with a slight nod, and closed the door.

I paced the hallway, unwilling to sit on the floor and unable to stand still. What was the man doing? Who could he call that I hadn't already checked in with? What did he know that I didn't? Probably lots of stuff, but at the moment, the only topic that mattered was Bruce.

After an interminable wait, that was in reality only a few minutes, Godwin's office door opened and the man emerged... and he did not look happy.

"I've found him," he practically growled. "I'll go retrieve him. You should go home."

"Where?" I yelped. "How? Is he all right?"

He waved a hand in the direction of the outside door. "Really, Miss Winters. You asked for my help and I'm helping. Now go home. This doesn't concern you."

"Doesn't concern me?" I asked, aghast at his arrogance. "You're talking about the man I love! My future husband!" I grabbed Godwin's arm to force him to face me. "I'm coming with you."

"You are not," he said, pulling free of my grasp. "You haven't a clue what's happening."

"Then you can enlighten me on the way," I snarled and stomped past him to the exit. "Hurry up. You're wasting time."

After a moment's hesitation, he strode past me, opened the exit, and motioned me outside.

"This isn't a good idea," he snapped, then took a deep breath, expelled it, and ushered me toward a brand new 1976 Cadillac Seville.

I stopped short, staring at the dark blue car. I didn't think that model was even available yet. My father owned a dealership and kept me up to date on the automotive world— whether I wanted to be or not. Where had Godwin gotten a Caddy that wasn't even available to the dealers yet?

Dr. Godwin was turning out to be quite the mystery.

Opening the passenger door for me, Godwin continued, "But

as you're soon to marry Bruce, you'll find out eventually. The boy won't be able to keep it from you forever."

I bristled at his description of Bruce as a boy. My fiancé was brilliant man. He might not have the physique of a body builder, but there was nothing boyish about him. He stood just over six feet tall, had wavy chestnut hair that he was constantly sweeping out of his gray-blue eyes, and was, to my eyes, the handsomest man on campus.

"Bruce is not..." I began, but Godwin spoke over me.

"You're going to learn some things that will test your belief system," he said as he backed out of the parking space and left the lot behind. "And you're going to need to trust me."

He glanced sideways at me before turning onto College Drive. "Can you do that?"

I nodded hesitantly, then, because he was watching traffic instead of me, added, "If it will help Bruce, sure." I waited a moment before asking, "Where are we going?"

"Conesus Lake."

I blinked. That was unexpected.

2

Ten minutes later— the longest ten minutes of my life!— we pulled into the parking area for Long Point Park. The crystal waters of Lake Conesus sparkled in the sunlight as we exited Godwin's Caddy.

"What are we doing here?" I asked. "I thought we were going to your cabin."

"You thought wrong," he said without so much as glancing at me. He walked to the edge of the water and stared out across the lake's placid surface. "Prepare yourself," he said. "Your education in the supernatural is about to begin."

I frowned, not having a clue what he was talking about, but joined him on the beach and braced myself.

Dr. Godwin looked around, as if to make sure we were alone, then stretched his right arm out over the water.

His arm changed.

I don't know what else to call it. One minute it was a normal guy's arm, complete with white dress shirt with the sleeve rolled up to his elbow, and the next it was covered in dark blue scales and ended in a clawed... foot?... instead of a hand.

I managed not to scream, but I did stumble back a few paces.

"I am here," he said, but not to me. "Come forth!"

Lake Conesus's still surface began to roil, losing its clear blue color as sediment was pulled from the depths. I fell back, landing solidly on my butt on the sandy beach, as a creature emerged from the foaming water. Whatever it was, it was a translucent silvery-blue and looked vaguely like a horse.

The word *kelpie* swam to the surface of my mind.

My undergrad degree was in literature. I'd studied Celtic mythology. I was familiar with the mythical water creature. What was a kelpie doing in the Finger Lakes of Upstate New York? Wait a minute— my brain caught up with my question— *kelpies were real?*

Before I even had a chance to scream, the creature— kelpie?— morphed into a young woman with flowing hair. Still the same translucent silvery-blue, she was dressed in a long, watery gown that disappeared into the frothy lake.

"You are prompt, my lord," she said, her voice a soft burble, cool against the day's growing heat. She glanced at me. "I'm surprised you brought another mortal when I already hold one of your pets."

Dr. Godwin shook his outstretched arm and it returned to normal flesh and blood. He glanced at me, frowned, and dismissed me. "She is nothing to me, but the boy… I require his services. What do you want?"

"Ahh," she said. "In that case, perhaps we should simply trade. You give me the female, and I'll return the male to you." She paused as she considered me, her head cocked to one side. "Yes. He's been much less entertaining than I'd hoped. Perhaps a female will suit my… needs… better."

"No," Dr. Godwin growled. "You shall have neither. They are a mated pair. And the male is mine." He glared at her as though he might vaporize the very mist she appeared to be made of. "No one," he said, slowly and with great menace, "steals from my hoard. Not if they wish their existence on this fair land to continue."

She rocked back at the threat. "Y-your hoard? You consider the male part of your hoard?"

"I do! Return him now or face the consequences."

She drew herself up, seeming to regain the composure she'd lost momentarily. "You have no power here. Water is not your element."

He grinned. A wicked expression I hoped never to see again. His eyes glinted with a red light and I swear smoke rose from his skin. "Not water, no."

Dr. Godwin hesitated, glanced once more in my direction, and suddenly the man vanished! In his place stood a massive, blue-scaled, fire-breathing dragon!

Flames shot from his gaping maw— a cavernous mouth, its opening large enough I could have stood in it— sweeping the watery figure away with its blast.

The kelpie screamed and dissolved into Lake Conesus.

I scuttled backward, crab-walking as far from the dragon as I could manage. What had Bruce gotten himself into? His major professor and mentor was a *dragon*? He'd been kidnapped by a *kelpie*? Was my fiancé even human? Was Bruce some kind of mythical creature too?

I choked on a sob, suddenly aware that tears streamed across my face.

"No tears," the dragon growled at me without even glancing in my direction. "Water is her element. She could use them against you."

I sniffled and dragged the hem of my peasant blouse across my face to dry it. "W-what d-do w-we d-do now?" I stammered. I was talking to a *dragon*! "Sh-she still has B-bruce!"

He closed his eyes, laid down on the sand with his forepaws tucked beneath his chest and his tail curled around his body, for all the world like a gigantic, scaly blue cat. A curious hum emitted from his throat, low enough that I felt the sand shift and shake beneath my trembling body. Smoke tendrils curled from his nostrils, dissipating into the clear blue summer sky.

Everything seemed normal. White puffy clouds floated overhead. Birds chirped in the trees beside the park's picnic tables. Wavelets lapped the beach where it joined the lake's waters. The air smelled fresh… except for the faint smoky odor of the… dragon!

Dr. Godwin was a *dragon*! Nothing would ever be normal again!

My stomach lurched and bile rose in my throat. I gagged… as quietly as I could. Retching might be considered adding to the enemy's store of water.

After a moment, the humming ceased and the dragon opened his eyes and turned their lamp-like focus on me. "You have handled this better than expected. Bruce chose well."

I almost thanked him, but choked on the words.

"Know this, though fire is *my* element, I am not the only dragon in the region. I have called a… clanmate… to aid us."

He turned his great head and stared across the water, calm again now that the kelpie was not in sight. After a moment, he cocked his head and gave me a side-eyed gaze.

"You should also know that Bruce, while fully human, is my familiar. He is bound to me and will never leave me. My magic requires his focus."

3

My pulse settled and I closed my eyes with a sigh of relief. My fiancé wasn't a monster. He was a human, just like me. Only...

I frowned.

Bruce was a *familiar*? Like a witch's cat?

What the heck did that even mean?

He'd never leave Godwin?

My eyes opened with a snap and I sat upright, my spine rigid. "You mean, if I marry Bruce, I'll be stuck with *you* until I die?" My voice got more shrill with each word until *die* was nearly beyond the range of human hearing.

But not dragon hearing.

The dragon actually winced.

"Calm yourself, Miss Winters. You won't be stuck with me until *you* die, only until *Bruce* passes from this realm."

"Oh," I huffed. *"That's* comforting!"

He silenced me with a glare and rose to his feet— all *four* of them! "She comes."

Expecting the kelpie's return, I scuttled back a few more feet until I could sit in the grass. Don't ask me why sitting on grass felt safer than sand, because I don't know. If you're ever on a beach with a dragon and a kelpie battling over your fiancé, you can let me know your thoughts on the matter.

But what rose from the water wasn't just the kelpie... a water dragon appeared from the depths of the churning water with the kelpie clamped in its jaws. The new creature didn't have scales, but smooth blue-green skin and luminous silver eyes. Instead of wings and legs ending in clawed feet, it sported massive flippers and a long sinuous neck.

"Nessie," I whispered.

Godwin-dragon turned to me. "Not Nessie," he growled, "but her close kin. She came to Conesus through a watery portal to help us. Now be silent, lest you offend her with your ignorance."

I nodded and zipped my lips. Anything to get Bruce back.

Not-Nessie spit the kelpie onto the surface of the water. "Flee at your peril," she said, her voice strangely musical.

Enchanting, really. I wanted nothing more than to obey her every stated wish. Godwin-dragon glanced at me and rolled his huge eyes. He breathed smoke across my face and Not-Nessie's spell washed away. I blinked as he returned his attention to the water creatures.

"Know that I am faster and far more powerful than you." Not-Nessie continued to admonish the kelpie. "There is nowhere you can hide."

The kelpie, in horse form once again, cowered on the lake's blue surface. "I am yours, mistress of the deep. Command me."

Not-Nessie glanced at Godwin-dragon. He cocked his head, and she nodded.

"You have taken something that does not belong to you, something of great value to my kinsman. Return it now and I shall not destroy you." Not-Nessie paused before finishing her thought. "Defy me at your peril."

The kelpie glared at Godwin-dragon, but bowed her head to Not-Nessie. "Of course, mistress. I will retrieve the human now."

She sank below the surface, but Not-Nessie stopped her

descent with a massive flipper, flinging her high into the air before she belly flopped on the surface once again.

"No," she said. "You will lead me to your captive. *I* will retrieve my kinsman's property."

Looking less silvery and more greenish, the kelpie wilted. "As you will, mistress. Follow me."

The two water creatures disappeared beneath Lake Conesus's sky-blue surface.

"Well," said Godwin-dragon, "that was well done. Time to get ready for Bruce's return." He glanced at me. "Kindly return to the car and fetch my extra set of clothes." He kicked up a bit of sand with his foreclaw. "The keys are there. The clothes are in the trunk." He eyed me critically. "And dust yourself off and straighten your hair. You look a fright."

I stood, snatched the keys from the sand, and stomped off to the parking area. I *looked a fright* indeed! Who was he to judge my appearance, after the morning he'd put me through? Ordering me around like some stupid lackey! Who would retrieve his clothes if I hadn't come along?

Oh. Never mind. If I wasn't along, he'd simply morph back into a man—evidently a *nude* man— and get them himself.

Fine.

I didn't want to see him in his birthday suit anyway. Eww!

I gathered his clothes, relocked the Caddy, and stomped back to the beach. "Here," I said, laying the fresh clothes on the grass at the edge of the beach. "I'll be over by the picnic table when you're decent again."

Would I ever consider him a *decent* man again? I didn't know, but it seemed that if I still intended to marry Bruce, I'd have to come to terms with Drake Godwin.

Did I still intend to marry Bruce?

I mulled that question over while I brushed sand off my bell-bottoms, straightened my blouse, and finger-combed my hair before pulling it back into a high ponytail. When Godwin called my name, I marched down to the edge of the water and, scooping a handful, washed the last traces of tears from my face.

There. That was the best I could do in the current circumstances. I shot a glance at Godwin's neatly dressed figure— white button-down shirt, black trousers, narrow blue plaid tie— and moved to stand beside him.

He turned to face me, studied my appearance, and nodded. "Much better. Bruce has had a trying experience. I don't want him upset by your dramatics. Do we understand each other?"

I closed my eyes and let his arrogance wash over me. I'd asked for his help, and he'd given it, albeit in a very unexpected way. Haughtiness aside, he was right. Bruce was the victim here, not me.

Opening my eyes, I met Godwin's gaze directly. "We do. As long as you understand that my relationship with Bruce is sacrosanct. It's ours, not yours. How we relate to each other is *none of your business*. Now or *ever*. Do we understand each other?"

He held my gaze a moment longer, then smiled. A very feral smile. "We do."

The water roiled, and forgetting our stand-off, we turned to greet my very water-logged fiancé.

Not-Nessie held Bruce aloft, her teeth clenched in his belt, and gently deposited him on the shore. "Your familiar, cousin."

Bruce fell to his hands and knees in the sand, coughing and spluttering. I ran to his side, pushing his hair out of his eyes and cupping his face in my hands.

"Are you all right?" I asked, searching his face for signs of damage.

"I'll survive," he said. Frowning, he looked from me to the water dragon conversing with Godwin. "What about you?"

I studied this man whom I loved— and knew without a doubt that dragons or no, he was the only one for me. I would deal with having a dragon named Drake Godwin in my life because Bruce was worth it. He was my everything.

I smiled. "I'm fine," I paused, then punched his soggy shoulder, "but don't ever keep secrets from me again! A dragon's familiar, indeed."

A chagrined look crossed his face. "I'm sorry. I should've told you."

Before I could utter a word, he pulled me into his arms and kissed me thoroughly. When we broke apart, he held me close and whispered, "I thought I'd never see you again. I love you, Lucy."

At that moment, an expensive loafer nudged us apart. "That's all very well and good," Dr. Godwin said, "but we should get back to campus. I have classes to teach."

"Yeah, yeah," I said, standing and pulling Bruce to his feet. "Everything is about you, isn't it?"

Godwin cocked an eyebrow at me before turning and walking to the Caddy. "Of course," he said. "Who else matters?"

Dragons! Arrogance personified.

Uncollected Anthology

A DIVERSITY OF DRAGONS

Issue 31 UA August 2023

HAVE HOARD, WILL SEEK

DEBBIE MUMFORD

1

Aidan Drake stared at his computer screen. Nothing. Again. This computer dating service sucked. Big time.

Leaning back in his ergonomically correct black leather executive chair, he stared at the unusually high ceiling of his home office. Painted deep blue and embedded with mica chips, it sparkled like the night sky... right where he wished he was at this moment.

Why was it so hard to find a mate in this modern world?

He was single, ruggedly handsome, and in possession of a well-tended hoard. What more could a female require? And yet, no matter how carefully he worded his profile. the online dating service only returned matches with obviously human women!

Where were the female dragons who were looking for love?

He couldn't be the only dragon-shifter in the Pacific Northwest who was ready to settle down and clutch some eggs, but it sure felt like it.

He'd tried bars and dance clubs, but while the strobing lights and wicked bass notes had filled his soul with primitive heat, he'd failed to find a worthy female. Actually, he'd failed to find *any* shifter females, worthy or otherwise.

He'd sampled the nightlife of cities all up and down the Pacific coast. From Vancouver, British Columbia and Seattle, Washington all the way south to San Diego, California. Even his beloved Portland, Oregon had left him flat... and still lonely.

It seemed Aidan was doomed to a loveless life.

He sat upright again, switched off his computer, and bounced to his feet. "Buck up, mate," he growled to himself. "You're not the first dragon to have trouble finding a mate and you won't be the last. You need something to take your mind off your troubles."

He paced the edges of his office, stopping occasionally to touch one of the pieces of his hoard on display in the room. An ancient sword, its blade kept as sharp as the day it was forged, its hilt glittering with precious stones; the golden chalice he'd wrested from an Aztec priest who'd tried to sacrifice Aidan to Huitzilopochtli—he smiled at the memory, that had been fun; and one of the famed golden apples of Atalanta. And these were only the small pieces he chose to display. His main hoard filled a magically warded cave in the Tualatin Mountains. He'd been adding to his hoard for centuries, moving it by enchantment to whatever country, or continent, he currently inhabited. All in anticipation of the moment when his mate would clutch their eggs in the nest of gold he'd built so carefully.

But now that all was in readiness, could he find a suitable mate? No!

The situation was absolutely untenable!

He resumed his pacing. He needed a distraction lest he burn down the entire luxury apartment building where he occupied the penthouse suite. And since he also owned the building, that wouldn't do at all. A fire would...

Wait a minute... that was it! Fire! Aidan needed a good, roaring blaze to combat his aggravation and agitation.

Fire! Where could he start a fire? Not a tame little combustion confined to a hearth, but a full-fledged conflagration. A living, breathing, inferno that consumed everything in its path. The eternal element that all dragons craved and loved.

But starting such a blaze was risky, especially since humans got all out of sorts when things starting burning in their vicinity. What he needed was a preexisting pyre. One he could revel in, but not be responsible for. A fire he could bask in without raising further human concern.

Racing back to his computer, he booted it up and began searching for wildfires. It was summer, surely he wouldn't have to fly far to find one. The news was usually full of reports of such burns at this time of year.

What luck! A wildfire was currently consuming hundreds of acres of land just across the Columbia River in Washington State's Gifford Pinchot National Forest.

Closing down the computer again, Aidan hurried to his private roof access. As soon as he stood beneath the starry sky, he stripped down, grabbed the backpack he kept packed with a change of clothes, water, and a few snacks, and transformed from man to dragon.

By the First Egg! It felt good to wear scales again. He'd been cooped up in human form for far too long. Clutching the pack in his front claws, he stretched his neck and gave his deep blue scales a quick once over. Check. He was in magnificent condition! With a bound, he spread his wings, launched into the night sky, and aimed for the wildfire.

He intended to thoroughly enjoy this blazing hot night.

2

Finding the blaze was no problem. As soon as he assumed his dragon form, Aidan's keen sense of smell detected smoke molecules floating in the night sky. Arrowing toward the Columbia, he sorted through the various flavors and followed the motes of burning timber. Pine resin and aspen sap rendered a flavorful combination unmistakable to his dragon senses. He relished the odor while delighting in the rush of cool night air over his scales.

He really needed to wear his dragon skin more often.

As long as he avoided airplanes— and how hard was that, when he could hear their roar from miles away, even the little ones?— the night sky was his. No one would see him, not when his dark blue scales blended so perfectly against the starry canopy. Besides, if a human did spot him, they'd simply decide he was an interestingly shaped cloud. Humans had always possessed an amazing talent for rationalization, explaining away anything that didn't fit in their very narrow perception of reality.

No, he was safe from human notice.

The glow of the raging wildfire soon lit the northern horizon. The closer he flew, the warmer the air became. When the leaping, crackling reds and oranges filled his visual field he scanned for fire lines. Though it was after midnight, firefighters still manned the fire break they'd created earlier in the day. Their vigilance amused him. They would eventually bring the blazing beast under control, but not before he had enjoyed its warmth and volatility.

Sweeping away from the watchers— who were busy watching the fire and missed the dragon soaring above them, even the *whoosh* of his wing strokes was masked by the roar of the flames — Aidan flew to the center of the devastation. He didn't worry about the firelight reflecting off his belly scales; there was no one here to see him. He hovered for a moment in midair, enjoying the dance of the flames below, and then allowed gravity to pull him into the fire's embrace.

The fire welcomed him. Flames licked his scales and danced along his snout and tail in wanton glee. They whispered their joy at his presence, knowing that he understood them, appreciated them.

Aidan relished their heat and destructiveness. Dragons and flames belonged to each other; they were kindred spirits. He rolled in their ash, delighting in the heat and roar of the inferno. Bliss filled his soul. He stilled his movement, closed his eyes, and basked in the warmth of the conflagration.

"Where did you come from?" a melodic voice asked.

Aidan startled. Opening his eyes he saw a young woman walking through the flames. It was hard to tell through the nimbus of orange and yellow that surrounded her, but he thought her hair was chestnut brown and her skin a warm, golden tan.

"Portland," he answered, awed by the knowledge that he had finally found a female shifter, for she could be nothing else. "And you?"

She shrugged. "Here and there. I follow the wildfires. The humans think I'm a smoke jumper." She laughed. "They have no clue that fire is my natural element and I can fly without a plane."

With that, she raised her head to the night sky and transformed into the most beautiful red dragon Aidan had ever seen. Her scales sparkled in the firelight and flames danced along her neck ridge and outstretched wings. She was magnificent, and Aidan wanted her more than any golden hoard he'd ever imagined.

"Who are you?" he growled, leaping to his feet. If she was to be his mate, he knew what came next; he needed to be ready.

"I am Aline," she said, studying him from snout to tail, "and I have been searching for you." Without another word, she unfurled her wings and leapt to the sky, the light of the flames reflecting from her scales. "Prove your worth," she called. "Catch me and I am yours!"

Aidan didn't hesitate. He launched into flight, his powerful wings beating the air and propelling him after the female he'd sought so diligently.

"I am Aidan," he bellowed after her fleeing form, "and I am worthy!"

Aline rose higher and higher into the velvet darkness of the night sky. She was powerful in flight, and her strength thrilled Aidan even as he fought to catch her. The higher they flew, the thinner the air became. Aidan's lungs burned, it had been too long since he'd exercised his wings. His stamina wasn't what it had once been.

But he refused to lose her. Not now that he had found her.

He dug deep into his fiery determination and shot ever higher. He would catch her! He would prove himself worthy! He'd searched too long to lose her in flight!

Slowly he gained on her, and when at last he pulled even with her, he saw that her color had dulled. She was tiring. This flight had been hard for her as well.

"Enough," he called, and using the last of his strength he positioned himself above her and turned her flight away from the stars and back to the glowing embers of the wildfire far below. As they descended, the air grew oxygen-rich and flying became easier. By the time they landed back in the fiery furnace of the burning forest, Aidan felt rejuvenated and Aline's scales glowed with health.

She cocked her head and studied him. "You are indeed a worthy male. I had despaired of finding you. Fire had become my only joy."

Aidan nodded. "I have searched up and down the Pacific Coast for a worthy female, and found nothing. Not even an unworthy candidate. It is fitting that we found each other in fire."

"Yes," she agreed. "You live nearby?"

"Across the river in Portland. Will you come with me?"

She glanced away, then met his gaze. "I will, though I do not yet accept you as mate."

He nodded. "I understand. We have much to discuss before such a decision is made."

"Yes," she said. "Lead. I will follow."

3

Aline sat comfortably curled at the end of Aidan's deeply cushioned, black leather couch. She wore the midnight blue bathrobe he'd provided when she emerged from the shower in the ensuite bath adjoining his guest bedroom. She had to admit, the man lived well in this penthouse suite, in a building he owned.

She'd been impressed by his dragon scales, both by his ability to endure the wildfire's flame and his prowess in flight. And the sight of his physical form had awed her. Blue scales shining in the firelight, his extensive wingspan, and the noble shape of his massive horned head. She shivered at the memory. She'd been forced to assume her own dragon form just to contain her admiration.

And now she admitted to herself that his human form was just as enticing. He sat across from her in a black leather recliner, his long legs stretched across the footrest, the picture of a human male at ease in his own home. Only this male wasn't human. He was a shifter, and the longer she was in his company, the more she thought he might be the mate she'd sought. His black hair shone with deep blue highlights, hinting at the color of his dragon's scales. Intelligence sparkled in his blue eyes and his chiseled features drew her as no human male's could.

They'd enjoyed a meal together after their demanding flight. One he'd prepared himself. Perfectly grilled steak, rare, of course, sliced tomatoes, potato salad, and lightly toasted garlic bread. He called it an *impromptu* meal. She called it a feast. Of course, he'd confided in her that he'd once spent a decade or two as the chef at an elegant French restaurant. The varied experiences of his life put her existence to shame. She'd spent most of her relatively young life chasing wildfires.

He'd survived the rigors of dragon-slaying knights, while she'd been clutched in the more gentle years of the nineteenth century.

As man or dragon, Aidan was intriguing and she genuinely enjoyed his company. He would make a fine mate. Except for one important detail. She'd seen only a few pieces of gold adorning his home. As decorations, they were lovely, but as a hoard, they were pathetic. And to think he'd had long centuries to accumulate wealth. Instead, he'd apparently wasted his time playing with humans.

Too bad. She'd had such high hopes when she came across him in the midst of the fiery furnace of the wildfire.

She rose to standing, stretched, and smiled at the male lounging in his recliner. "Well, this has been lovely, Aidan, but dawn is approaching and it's time for me to go lest I be seen flying home."

"You're more than welcome to stay," he said, lowering the footrest and jumping to his feet. "I can send someone to your home to retrieve your clothes. The guest bedroom is at your disposal for as long as you'd like."

He didn't beg, but the tremor in his voice told her exactly how much he longed for her to stay. The longing was mutual. But much as she liked and admired him, she couldn't mate with a dragon who didn't possess a respectable hoard.

She shook her head. "I appreciate the offer," she said quietly, but firmly, "but this will not do. I cannot accept you as a mate."

His expression darkened and his brows lowered in a frown. "Is there a reason? I thought we were getting along well. I even detected a... spark... between us."

She sighed. "Yes. I felt it too, but you are unprepared for a mate."

His brows shot up, his eyes widening. "Unprepared? How so? I am wealthy beyond human understanding and I own this building. You and our hatchlings would want for nothing!"

"Perhaps," she agreed, lowering her gaze and moving to place the couch between them. She had no desire to deal with an enraged shifter male, but...

"However, I've seen no hoard. I cannot clutch eggs without an appropriate nest of gold to nurture my young. How would they thrive? Gold, and large amounts of it, are necessary to a hatchling's health. Surely you know this." She glanced around the room. "Your trinkets are lovely, but they are inadequate to the needs of a nesting dragon and her clutch of eggs."

To her surprise, Aidan laughed. A relieved and carefree sound that danced around the room and lifted her spirits. "Truly?" he asked. "Is that your only concern? My lack of a hoard?"

Now Aline frowned. "Isn't it enough?" she asked. "As I said, you are unprepared for a mate."

"I am not," he growled. "I have spent centuries preparing, and now that I am ready, I have spent decades in my search for a mate. I hoped you would be she, but as you are unprepared to trust me, I suppose I shall have to continue my search."

"Trust you?" Aline gasped. "How have I failed to trust you? I led you on a proving flight, which you passed magnificently I might add, and followed you to your home expecting to find a true dragon's hoard, not a human male's bachelor pad! You have deceived me!"

"Deceived you?" Aidan roared. "I have told you nothing but

the truth. I caught you in flight. I brought you to my home. I sheltered you and fed you and answered every question you asked. Yet you failed to ask the one that mattered most: the location of my hoard."

He drew himself up to his full height, fury written on his features. "I thought you young and flighty not to ask, but instead you are merely stupid and judgmental. What sensible dragon would live with his hoard in this modern age? I enjoy my comforts here, while my hoard is safely warded and hidden. Deep in the hills, in a cave, as it should be."

Aline stepped back around the couch and crumpled against its cushioned seat. "You have a hoard?" she whispered.

Aidan sat back down, but did not relax into his recliner. "Of course I have a hoard. Why else would I invite you here and attempt to get to know you?"

The silence in the room was deafening. But neither shifter broke it. Both were lost in their own bleak thoughts. They'd had a chance. Was mating now beyond their reach?

At last, Aidan broke room's quiet. "I apologize for calling you stupid and judgmental."

Aline nodded. "And I apologize for assuming you were unprepared to mate."

"It seems we've been at cross-purposes. Would you consider trying again?"

She glanced up and met his blue-eyed gaze. "I would. I will fly home now, but I would enjoy seeing you again."

"That would please me as well."

Both stood, and Aidan walked her to the roof where she gave him her cell phone number before transforming and flying away into the lightening sky.

4

Aidan fidgeted behind the steering wheel of his deep blue Mazarati GranTurismo. Aline would be joining him any moment now, and he was more nervous than he'd ever been in his centuries-long life. They'd been dating for nearly three months, and he was certain she was the shifter for him. Not only was her ruby red dragon form gorgeous, but she made an impressive human female as well. Long, red-highlighted chestnut hair. Lovely hazel eyes. Finely sculpted cheekbones and chin. And a lush, curvaceous form that drove his human form mad with longing.

They'd made no commitments yet, but Aidan had high hopes, and today... today would determine their fate as a couple. He was about to take her to his hoard. Everything rested on her reaction to the gold he'd been accumulating for centuries.

Female dragons didn't hoard gold— that was the male's responsibility— but females required a vast amount of gold to safely clutch their eggs, and when those eggs hatched, the infant dragons required gold to grow and mature in health. Everything in a dragon's long life centered on gold, and Aidan was about to find out if his preparations had been adequate to his potential mate's needs and expectations.

The passenger door opened and Aline slid into the seat beside Aidan. She smiled, kissed his cheek, and asked, "Ready?"

He took a deep breath, exhaled it, and nodded. "As I'll ever be."

She fastened her seat belt. "Then let's do this."

They travelled in silence until Aidan turned off Skyline Boulevard onto Newton Road and then into a small parking area for a Forest Park trailhead. Aline glanced at him in question, but exited the car and looked around. The air was fresh, smelling of green growing things, pine resin, and just a hint of car exhaust. The day was gorgeous— clear blue skies sprinkled with a few white puffy clouds, with a gentle breeze wafting through the surrounding trees. Old growth trees, their branches reaching for the sun. The only thing that would've made the day better would've been the scent of smoke and burning sap.

Aidan led her toward the trees. Not to the well-established trailhead, but off to the side near where he'd parked the Mazarati. They dodged branches, skirted undergrowth, and stepped over exposed roots and the occasional downed tree limbs for about fifteen minutes before he ushered her into a clearing of knee high grasses and dappled sunlight.

"We're here," he announced. "Mind you, you'd never find your way here again without my permission."

Aline glanced around the clearing. "It's a beautiful spot, but there's nothing here."

Aidan smiled and waved his hands. "Oh really?"

The air shimmered and the trees on one side of the clearing disappeared. In their place stood a rocky outcropping with a large crevasse that opened onto darkness.

Aline stepped back in surprise, then nodded. "Very nicely done. Your wards are impressive."

"Thank you. My wards have never been breached, and I've been protecting this hoard for centuries."

Aline's smile warmed him like flame. "I can hardly wait to see what you've gathered."

He held out his hand. "Then come with me."

She clasped hands with him and they stepped into the dark. Together.

They were barely past the entrance when the rock walls widened into a cavern of immense proportions. Much too large to be sheltered beneath the outcropping they'd seen from the outside. The floor was smooth and sandy, which in itself was odd since the soil in Forest Park was loam and clay. The walls and ceiling, though clearly rock, looked as though they'd been melted in a high heat. But the most amazing thing was the hoard itself. A wide depression in the back of the cave was piled high with gold. All manner of gold. Coins. Jewelry. Goblets and plates. Even pieces of armor sparkled in the unnatural light that emanated from Aidan himself.

Aline stepped forward and knelt beside the huge pile of treasure. Plunging her hands in, she let the coins run through her fingers. She rose and stepped into the hoard, smiling as her eyes closed, a blissful expression on her face.

She turned to Aidan. "May I?"

He inclined his head and performed a small bow. "As you wish, my lady."

Aline stripped off her clothes and transformed.

Aidan smiled. He'd prepared well. There was plenty of room in the cave for a dragon. No. For two dragons. He shed his own clothes, transformed, and joined Aline in the hoard. The shifter he'd come to love was busily excavating a nest in his hoard. The sight filled him with both pride and delight.

He nuzzled her lovely scaled cheek. "Will it do, Aline?"

She turned her head and gazed into his eyes, happiness evident in her features. "Do? Oh, Aidan, it's a perfect hoard! If you'll have me, we'll clutch many healthy offspring in this place."

Aidan's head reared back in surprise. "If I'll have you? Aline,

I've wanted you since the first moment I saw you surrounded by flames! You are the mate I've prepared for all these long, lonely years."

Aline sighed in contentment, a small gout of flame bursting from her nostrils. Closing her eyes, she leaned her head against his shoulder. "You accept me," she nuzzled against his deep blue scales, "and I accept you. We are mates."

Aidan rested his chin against the top of her head. "We are mates," he agreed. "Together for eternity."

"Together," she echoed, "for eternity."

Aidan closed his eyes and relaxed. It had been a long, lonely wait, but Aline, his one and only mate, was *so* worth it.

ENCHANTMENT, INC.

DEBBIE MUMFORD

BESTSELLING AUTHOR OF *SORCHA'S CHILDREN*

1

I raced through the expansive lobby of Enchantment, Inc., pushing past gawking tourists and weaving among guests of the massive complex. Humans! Completely oblivious to my fear, and their own danger at the hands, and claws, of the goons who hunted me.

How could they see the soaring vault of the atrium's crystal ceiling, the lacy balcony railings of the three floors of boutique shops, restaurants, and theaters that overlooked the atrium lobby and not know that magic was involved? Enchantment, Inc. might exist in Las Vegas, Nevada, but it was owned, operated, and supported by the Realm of Faery, and I'd done the unthinkable. I'd defied a direct order from the Dark King.

My very existence was forfeit unless I managed to reach the top of the complex before the goons—trolls wearing human glamours—caught me.

I reached a bank of elevators and paused. Did I dare enclose myself in a metal box to reach the upper floors? I glanced over my shoulder, saw the grinning face of a hobgoblin, and thought better of it. Hobgoblins had an affinity for metal. If I stepped inside that car, I'd never emerge again. Not with my human form intact.

I dodged past guests waiting for the elevator and ran for the escalators instead.

By the First Egg! Why had I defied the king? What did I care if the construction of a rival's hotel / entertainment complex collapsed in an inferno of dragon fire?

If only I could shift into my natural shape, leave this human form behind! As a dragon, I could rise to the top of Enchantment, Inc. on powerful wings. In my natural form, trolls and hobgoblins, even the Dark King himself, were no match for me!

Unfortunately, I was a citizen of Faery and subject to the commands of the king and queen. When the king laid a geas on me, my magic could only obey. I could no more shift than one of the human tourists who crowded the atrium pointing out its wonders could.

My heartbeat drummed as I jumped on the escalator and wove through the other passengers, desperate to reach the second floor before the goons found me.

I glanced up and saw two of the trolls cracking their huge knuckles at the top of the escalator. Their glamours made them appear as very large human males. Bald, poured into dark blue suits that stretched across heavily muscled chests and shoulders, but I saw beyond the glamours. I saw their gray-green hides, tusks protruding from the corners of cavernous mouths, and thick, clawed fingers and toes.

I paused in my upward trajectory and glanced around for options.

There were none.

Wearing this frail human form, I couldn't jump off the escalator. I'd break an arm or a leg and the goons on the atrium floor would be on me in a flash.

I couldn't transform and fly to safety. The king's geas had seen to that.

I couldn't push past the people lining the escalator treads below me and run for the exit. There were no exits for me. The king's geas had also sealed all of the exits against me. I was trapped within this complex, and huge as it was, they'd find me eventually.

Heck, they'd found me now. The escalator was delivering me straight into their meaty paws.

I had to think, and quickly, the remaining escalator treads were disappearing faster than I cared to consider. Think! I might be trapped in human form, but I was still a dragon. An apex predator. Quick and agile and, above all, intelligent.

Trolls were none of those things.

A plan glimmered into being, and I stood straight, muscles loose and ready for action.

Smiling at the king's goons, I lagged behind the family stepping off the escalator just ahead of me. As the trolls stepped back to allow the man, woman, and three kiddies space, I ran forward two steps, dropped to the floor, and let my minuscule momentum carry me past the trolls heavy feet.

Rolling over, I lunged to my feet and ran, dodging between gawking tourists, narrowly avoiding pushing one young man over the railing and to his death on the atrium floor. Human remains splattered on the pristine marble floors would only enrage the already angry king.

The second floor of the complex held a myriad of food establishments. Anything a human could want to eat could be found here. From casual food courts featuring hot dogs, hamburgers, and pizza by the slice, to haute cuisine restaurants with fine china, crystal goblets, and sterling silver flatware.

In a desperate attempt to lose the goons now hot on my heels, I barged into an Italian restaurant complete with red checked tablecloths and candles in chianti bottle holders and ran straight through, past surprised waitstaff and wide-eyed customers, to the kitchen.

As soon as I passed the swinging doors, the smell of frying meat, rich tomato sauce replete with onions and garlic, hit my nostrils. My mouth watered and my stomach growled. I hadn't eaten since last night, but couldn't stop now. Not when the goons would push through those same swinging doors in a matter of seconds.

I did manage to grab a piece of thick, crusty bread as I sprinted out the rear exit into the service hallways. These passages were used for catering and room service deliveries. No need for the guests to see the inner workings of the complex's food service industry.

The empty hallway gave me the opportunity to speed ahead without dodging humans. I stuffed the bread into my mouth and chewed as I rushed toward a bank of service elevators. A quick glance around told me I was alone. No hobgoblins to make this a mistake. Besides, I'd have to brave the crowded guest corridors if I wanted to make it back to the escalators.

No options.

I had to get to the infinity pool on the roof if I was to survive, and since I couldn't fly, I needed the elevator.

The doors slid open, revealing a waiter in black slacks and vest with a pristine white shirt and an empty service cart. He frowned at me, but shrugged and stepped off, moving to one side so I could enter the car unimpeded.

I turned to face the opening and, as the doors slid shut, saw the trolls lumbering down the hallway toward me.

Breathing a sigh of relief, I slumped against the car's walls and caught my breath. The car hurtled upward, bypassing floors of boutique shops and entertainment venues, heading non-stop to the rooftop access.

If I could just make it to the infinity pool, I could present my petition to the Queen of Air and Light who held court there. She was the Dark King's equal. If she blessed me with her favor, I could return to the Realm of Faery and my clan's aerie.

If I made it home, I'd never venture into the mortal world again. No matter what inducements Enchantment, Inc. might offer. I'd also caution my clan against signing up. Not without significant riders to the standard contract.

But first I had to survive.

The elevator dinged and the doors slid open to the rooftop where the infinity pool and the queen's court waited...

...to reveal not one, not two, but six goons blocking my access to the queen and her court!

I'd made it to the roof, but my flight had been in vain. I was doomed.

With a frantic surge of energy, I plowed in amongst the trolls, screaming for the queen's attention.

"My lady," I cried. "My liege! I beg sanctuary!"

The trolls grabbed my arms, my shoulders, and pushed me back into the elevator car.

If the doors closed before the queen acknowledged me, my life was over.

"Please," I screamed. She had to hear me. The queen was my only hope! "Great Queen, I beg you!"

The doors slid shut and I slumped into the trolls' muscular and uncaring embrace, knowing that their musky stink and tusked faces would be my last perceptions.

2

_____

A slender hand slipped into the gap just before the elevator entrance sealed shut. The doors automatically retracted revealing a slender elf knight wearing traditional green tunic and leggings, his silver blond hair tucked neatly behind his pointed ears.

He glanced at my captors. "Bring him," he said, and stepped aside.

The trolls glanced at each other, shrugged, and half dragged, half pushed me out of the elevator car and toward the infinity pool.

Arriving at the edge, the goons pushed me to my knees and stepped away, joining the members of the queen's court who lounged around the pool, soaking in the light of the summer sun. A few of her maids rested in the shallows of the infinity pool, close enough to answer a summons, but far enough to allow their lady peace and tranquility.

I raised my face and saw the glory of the Queen of Air and Light.

She floated on the water, reclining on a giant lily pad, with a view of the entire cityscape of Las Vegas spread out at her feet. The pool seemed to disappear into the air, limitless and serene.

The queen herself was beauty incarnate, emerald green eyes, porcelain complexion, and perfect, delicate features. She wore a long gown of gauzy blue-green fabric that shimmered in the summer sun and a delicate golden circlet held back her silver blonde hair.

"You begged sanctuary," she said, her voice clear and musical. "You have my attention. Speak your request."

I licked my lips and swallowed. Hard. I'd only get one chance. If I misspoke and she flicked her wrist, there would be no reprieve.

"Great Queen," I said, struggling to keep my voice calm and even, "my liege, the Dark King, has placed a geas on me. I cannot leave Enchantment, Inc. and I cannot transform into my natural state. I am captive and hunted by trolls."

I paused, closed my eyes, and gathered my thoughts for my final petition.

"I humbly beseech you to lift the geas and allow me to return to the Realm of Faery."

The queen cocked her head and studied me, a slight frown marring her exquisite features.

"What is your natural form?"

"I am a dragon of the Ice Aerie, Great Queen."

"And why are you in the mortal world?"

"I signed a contract to work for Enchantment, Inc. for the space of one year, my lady."

"And what were the terms of your contract?"

I lowered my eyes, feeling my heart sink. The bread I'd eaten so hurriedly sat like a lump of lead in the pit of my stomach. There would be no return to my aerie. Still, I raised my eyes and straightened my spine. The truth must be spoken.

"Obedience to the Dark King's commands, my lady," I said, knowing the words sealed my fate. The Fae lived by contract. One's word was one's bond. Our people were very careful with their words, whether written or spoken.

She frowned again, tapping one finger against her perfect lips.

"Since you are under the king's geas, I must assume you failed to obey a command." She paused.

As she had neither asked me a direct question nor sent me away, I held my silence while she considered my plight.

"Still," she said after a moment, "you begged sanctuary. You must feel there were extenuating circumstances." She gave me a quizzical look, and I managed to nod. "I will hear your plea," she said, sitting up. The lily pad transformed into a throne of green vines scattered with small pink and white flowers, the whole still floating on the pool's shimmering blue surface.

"State your case, Sir Dragon. If your cause is just, I will release you from your bondage." She paused and lowered her softly melodic voice to a near growl. "But understand this, if I do release you, you will return to Faery where you will be barred from ever entering the mortal realm again."

I nodded. "I understand, majesty, and will accept your decision, whatever it may be." I closed my eyes and considered how to best tell my tale.

3

Truth. That was the essence of my plea. Every word I spoke must be true and above reproach. The Queen of Air and Light would know if I spoke a lie. Even if my words merely skirted the truth.

I glanced around at her courtiers. Elves. Sprites. Brownies. Even a few dwarves. All eyes rested on me. Her people would abide by their lady's decision, but they would judge me as well.

"My lady," I said, "it is true that I signed the contract requiring my obedience, but nowhere did the document state that the Dark King would require me to harm humans or rain death and destruction on their edifices."

I swallowed and licked my lips. "I realize now that I was naïve not to ask for an amendment specifying that such acts were beyond my scope, but I had not heard that harm to humans was allowed by Enchantment, Inc. Citizens of Faery might be disciplined for allowing harm to befall guests or tourists, but it was my belief and understanding that humans were to be protected at all costs."

The queen spoke before I could continue. "The Dark King commanded you to harm a human?"

I took a deep breath, held it for a moment, then expelled it with my words. "Not directly, my lady," I said. Honesty was paramount. "But he commanded me to destroy a large building complex that is under construction. The site is extensive. I could not be positive that no humans would be onsite and, as your majesty is well aware, dragon fire is deadly and unstoppable once set in motion."

She nodded, her frown deepening. She was about to speak when the elevator doors swooshed open and the Dark King strode forth. He swept to my side, grabbed my shoulder and yanked me to my feet.

"How dare you trouble my queen with your petty grievances," he growled, his handsome face a mask of fury. Dark as his queen was light, the king was dressed in a black business suit, complete with black silk shirt. His black, wavy hair fell across his deep brown eyes, and his deep, Mediterranean tan fairly glowed with a flush of anger.

I held my silence, awaiting the death curse he would surely deliver.

"Hold!" The queen strode across the pool, her bare feet barely skimming the water. The king pulled me back from the edge, giving his queen a place to stand. She glared at her king.

"Did you really order this dragon to destroy a human construction site?"

The king glared at me, but did not so much as glance at his queen. "It will be a viable competitor when complete," he growled. "I wish it not to be."

The queen snorted, a most indelicate sound from one so fair. "And you think Enchantment, Inc. with all its magic and Faery creatures will be unable to compete with a merely human complex?"

He glowered at her, but did not respond.

The queen nodded. "I see." She turned to her court with a sweeping gesture that included the king, his goons, and me. "I have made my decision. I find in favor of the dragon." She turned to her king. "You will lift the geas. All of them."

"Fine," he growled, waving his fingers at me. I felt a tightness lift from my spirit and knew that my ability to shift had been restored.

The queen then turned to me. "I would amend my ruling about banishing you from the human realm. Your old contract is null and void." She glanced at the king.

He waved his hand and the document appeared. After allowing the queen, and me, to inspect it, he lit it on fire and scattered its ashes to the wind.

The queen nodded.

Relief spread through my entire body. I was free. I could return to the Ice Aerie and live out my days in peace, making sure no other dragon ever faced the dilemma that had almost cost my life.

However, the Queen of Air and Light had other ideas about my future.

EPILOGUE

"Sir Dragon," the queen said, regaining my full attention. "If you are willing, I would like to draw up a new contract for your services."

"What?" shouted the king, while my eyebrows rose and my eyes widened in surprise.

The queen nodded. "This incident has highlighted Enchantment Inc.'s need for a new executive, one who is in charge of the ethical actions of the citizens of Faery. We have power that the humans are both unaware of and have no defense against. It is incumbent upon us to act responsibly toward them. Saying we will not harm guests or tourists is not sufficient."

She glared at the Dark King before continuing. "We need an officer whose sole duty it is to hold us to a higher standard." She turned to me. "I can think of no better candidate for the job than you, Sir Dragon. If you are willing to forego returning to your aerie."

I bowed my head and knelt before my queen. "I would be honored, your majesty." I looked up into her lovely face and smiled. "Of course, I reserve the right to study the document carefully and negotiate the wording if necessary."

She laughed, a delightful sound reminiscent of wind chimes in a summer breeze. "I would expect nothing less, Sir Dragon."

I breathed a sigh of relief. Not only had I survived, I had improved my standing in the queen's court. I was more than content.

AN ALIEN ADVENTURE

A DEEP SPACE
SHORT STORY

DEBBIE MUMFORD

1

Neila walked briskly through the gray and white plasteel corridors of the security sector of *The Great Beyond*, the generational ship that had been her only home. Head held high, clutching her midnight blue exo-helmet to her chest, she nodded to those she passed with what she hoped was serene calm.

She felt anything but!

Her belly jumped with excitement, alternating between happy flutters of anticipation and a roiling nausea that threatened to expel the light lunch she'd consumed barely an hour ago.

Her mother had chided her for not eating a more substantial meal, saying that Neila would need energy for the landing, but the mere smell of grilled meat made her queasy. Even the bread and cheese had hit her belly like bricks. No way she could've managed more.

With her mother's help, she'd donned her exo-suit. She'd worn one before, of course. Everyone on *The Great Beyond* was required to get into the skin-tight protective gear at least once a quarter. Captain Atherton, a third generation bridge officer, made sure the inhabitants of her ship were ready for any emergency. Her people wouldn't be laid low by native pathogens should they ever be forced to evacuate.

But this was the first time Neila would *need* an exo-suit. She'd come of age last month and her newly adult status placed her on rotation for planet-side exploration. Today was her day; her first chance to plant her feet on something besides *The Great Beyond*'s plasteel decking. She was going to touch down on a planetary surface!

Heart racing, Neila sucked in a deep, calming breath, and winced at the exo-suit's constraint. It didn't hurt, but it was tight. So very different from the loose tunics and soft leggings she usually wore.

She met a young man's gaze and blushed to the roots of her close-cropped dark hair. Honestly! It was like walking around naked, except nothing jiggled. The exo-suit kept her flesh too constricted for anything as normal as jiggling.

The guy nodded and walked on. Evidently exo-suited females were nothing out of the ordinary for him.

Neila rounded a bend and stopped before the hatch to the shuttle bay. Pushing a fist against her jumpy belly, she willed herself to icy calm. This was it. Her moment to prove herself. She would not vomit in front of the away team. She would behave professionally, with a calm beyond her years.

Palming the access panel, she stepped into the bay.

Captain Atherton glanced up as Neila entered, nodded and clapped her hands. The twenty-or-so exo-suited crew members immediately formed into neat lines, with Neila and two others scrambling to find places.

"Good afternoon, team." The captain met the eyes of each crew member. A short stocky woman, she exuded calm and control. "You have been assigned to explore the surface of G-4873, the planet we are now orbiting. Most of you have been on exploration teams before, but we have three newbies joining the ranks today. We all know that classes can only provide a minimum of preparation. The real learning takes place in the field. So teach the newbies what they need to know and bring them back safely."

She turned to the green exo-suited officer beside her. "Lieutenant Dreeson, you have command. Good hunting."

Lt. Dreeson saluted and waited while the captain exited the shuttle bay.

"All right, team. Let's get to work. Corporals Hoskins, Song, and Lomidze, take charge of your assigned newbies. The rest of you, let's get the gear on the shuttle."

Neila watched in confusion as the team erupted into action. She briefly considered moving to stand near the other two midnight-blue suited team members, the only other people looking as bewildered as she felt, but before she could move a green-suited woman approached her.

"Citizen Neila Spiros?" When Neila nodded, the woman continued. "I'm Corporal Ginny Song. Welcome to the exploration team."

Neila nodded, her mouth too dry to attempt speech.

Cpl. Song took Neila's elbow and guided her out of the bustle of activity.

"A few basics. Notice the different colors of exo-suits. Military crew wear green." She indicated her own exo-suit. "We're the most highly trained for combat and provide security for the rest of the team. Once you've passed your field tests, you'll be issued a side-arm, but you'll still rely on the greenies for optimal protection."

Neila swallowed, but nodded. "Got it. Green for guards."

Song smiled. "Exactly. The white suits are scientists; the blue are grunts." She cocked her head when Neila startled. "That is, regular citizens with no particular aptitude for planet-side duty. Those of you in the really dark blue are newbies. Once you pass your field tests, you'll be issued a new suit in the proper color."

"I'm studying biology," Neila said, "specializing in botany, though I'm taking a few courses in zoology. But even when I complete my coursework, I won't qualify as a scientist. At least, not for years."

Song nodded. "Then you'll be issued a yellow suit. Botany is considered a necessary planet-side skill, and our techs wear yellow."

"No techs today?"

"Correct. The make-up of our away team fluctuates depending on who's available and what the head science officer expects us to encounter." Song glanced around. "Looks like we're about ready to leave. Remember, when we get to the surface, stick to me. Don't go wandering off on your own."

"Yes, sir."

Song grinned. "That's the spirit, but I'm not an officer. You can call me Song."

Neila relaxed enough to smile. "Thank you, Song."

~

2

Neila's eyes widened when she stepped off the shuttle. She'd seen pictures of planets, of course. Everything from sand dunes to oceans to craggy mountains, but the experience of stepping onto a springy surface of leaf litter and loam was just... unreal.

Her exo-suit and helmet protected her from the environment, but still she could almost smell the life around her. The shuttle had landed in a long, narrow valley edged by tall plants that could only be described as purple trees. Their trunks, an unexpected lilac shade, rose high above the shuttle before branching out into an interlocking canopy of deep purple. The vegetation growing around their bases was quite varied. Some 'bushes' were deep green with what appeared to be thick, fleshy leaves, and some were shades of rose with delicate, feathery fronds.

All were fascinating and Neila's fingers itched for a sketch pad. But she wasn't here to take notes on botanical specimens, she was here to learn from Cpl. Song.

"Close your mouth, citizen," Song said, tapping Neila's shoulder, "and follow me."

During the shuttle ride Lt. Dreeson had given the team

assignments for their explorations. Song and Neila were assigned to assist a white-suited geologist, Dr. Ambrogi.

"I want soil samples," Dr. Ambrogi said. "We'll take the first here in the landing meadow." He pulled a long narrow metallic tube from his pack and handed it to Song. "You take the first one; show the newbie how it's done."

"My name is Neila, Doctor."

He cocked his head at her, then continued pulling equipment from his pack. "Fine. Show *Neila* how it's done, Corporal."

Song turned away from Ambrogi to hide her grin and motioned Neila down beside her in the dirt. "Nothing hard about this. Just stick the tube in the ground and depress the button on the top. You'll feel it vibrate. When it stops, pull it out and give it back to the doc."

Neila watched the process, noting that Ambrogi held the tube to his scanner and typed in a few notes before settling it into a fitted slot in a special compartment of his pack.

They repeated the sampling several times when they reached the tree line. Ambrogi required samples from beneath each species of 'tree' and 'bush,' though he seemed uninterested in the vegetation itself.

After an hour of slowly moving into the dense foliage, they lost sight of the other members of the team. Neila glanced up. The deep purple canopy was so thick she couldn't see the mauve sky, though a few shafts of greenish sunlight did pierce the vegetation.

Wait! What was that?

A flicker of movement caught her eye and she used the zoom feature of her exo-helmet's screen. Something glittered in a shaft of sunlight. Something flying.

She zoomed in again, noting the display's estimation of distance.

Whatever it was, it was sizable. She shouldn't have been able to pick it out from the ground without the zoom. Not when it was nearly 100 meters above her.

She shook her head. According to the display, the canopy of the purple trees was 150 meters up. Unbelievable. Especially when her textbooks said that the canopy of the giant redwood trees back on earth had only been about 30 or 40 meters off the ground. These tree-things were massive.

Just as she was about to apprise Song of her discovery, the creature dove for the forest floor. Right at Neila!

"Incoming!" She closed her eyes, ducked, and covered her head.

"Neila?" Song's voice echoed through her helmet. "What's wrong?"

Before she could answer, strong talons gripped her shoulders and yanked her upward.

3

Neila opened her eyes and closed them again quickly, her stomach heaving. The ground was so far below that Song and Ambrogi looked like ants. She fought to control both fear and nausea. Vomiting in an exo-helmet was so not a good idea!

Whatever this creature was, she sure hoped it didn't plan to drop her. Even with the protective shielding on her suit, Neila knew she'd splat like a raw egg if she hit the ground from this height.

She'd been briefed on how to respond if approached by an alien species, but not on what to do if snatched from the surface and hauled into an unbelievably high canopy.

What was this creature doing? Was she about to become dinner for a gang of its hungry young?

"Neila! Can you hear me?" Song called, her voice sounding even more tinny than usual through the suit's speakers. "Answer me, newbie!"

"I-I'm alive, Song. Wh-whatever this creature is, we're still flying." She opened her eyes again... and swallowed bile. "W-we're really high up. I sure hope this thing is friendly!"

"Friendly," echoed Song. "Yeah. Friendly would be good. Hang in there, Neila. Lt. Dreeson is on the way and *The Great Beyond* has been notified."

Like that's going to do me a lot of good! Neila closed her eyes against the nausea and allowed herself to go limp in the alien's claws.

A moment later the claws released her.

Vertigo hit hard as she fell, undoubtedly to her doom.

But the sensation only lasted an instant before she landed on something solid.

Neila's eyes popped open and she found herself sitting on a branch. A smooth, level branch as wide as a ship's corridor, and she was surrounded by...

...dragons?

She frowned and shook her head, but the creatures still looked like miniature dragons. About as long as she was tall, scaly, with crocodilian heads, leathery wings, two taloned feet, and long spiky tails.

Sun and stars she hoped they were...

"Friendly!"

She turned to face the one that she thought had brought her here. Had that dragon... creature... thing... just screeched the word *friendly*?

"Did you say something?"

"Friendly," it repeated, cocking its head and gazing into her eyes.

Neila stared back... and saw intelligence sparkling in those deep, dark amber pools.

Seriously, could these things be sapient? Could she, Neila Spiros, total newbie, be making first contact with an intelligent alien species?

Yes, said a melodic voice in her mind. *Welcome, Neila Spiros, total newbie, to Omneth. We are the People of the Quarnath, what you think of as 'purple trees.'*

H-How can I understand you? she wondered, staring wildly

around at the five dragons surrounding her. One was reddish purple, another dusky gray, the third was greenish gold, the fourth was a deep ocher, and the one that had snatched her from the ground and flown her to wherever the hell they were was the deep purple-black of a bad bruise. Only shiny. And sparkly where the sun touched its scales.

Qunum heard your words as you flew, one of them said, though she still had no idea which. *When your souls connected, our thoughts linked.*

Neila shook her head and said aloud, "Our *souls* connected? What the… heck… does that mean?"

The ocher dragon shuffled its feet and Neila turned to face it.

You… looked into Qunum's eyes. You saw him. He saw you. Your souls connected.

"But I didn't look into your eyes, and you're talking to me."

The bruise-colored dragon shuffled, and she turned back to him. Qunum, she supposed.

We are the People of the Quarnath, he said. *What one knows, all know. Is this not true of your people?*

Her eyes widened and her jaw dropped. She shook her head snapped her mouth shut. After a moment, she answered. "Definitely not."

"Citizen Neila Spiros," said a new voice through Neila's helmet speaker. "This is Captain Atherton. Are you well?"

Neila breathed a sigh of relief before responding. "I'm fine, Captain. I'm somewhere in the canopy having a nice chat with a few representatives of the People of the Quarnath." She glanced at Qunum. "I don't think they mean to harm me. They're friendly."

"That's good to know, Citizen. Ask if they will return you to the surface. We'll have a delegation ready to meet with them. Since we're guests on their planet, we need to establish a few rules."

Neila nodded, though the captain couldn't see her. "Understood, Captain. I'm sure they'll be amenable."

After a moment's silence, Capt. Atherton said, "Well done, Neila. You've had quite the experience for your first away team mission."

"Sir. It's been an adventure," she replied, glancing around at the small dragon-like creatures surrounding her, "and I wouldn't have missed it for the world!"

ALSO BY DEBBIE MUMFORD

Kristi Lundrigan Mysteries:

- DELECTABLE MOUNTAIN QUILTING (NOVEL)
- IN A PICKLE (NOVEL)
- DOUBLE WEDDING RING (NOVEL)
- FOOL'S PUZZLE (SHORT STORY)
- WILDFIRE! (SHORT STORY)
- CHRISTMAS STAR (SHORT STORY)

Sheriff Reynolds Mysteries:

- ABDUCTED! (NOVEL - PREORDER TODAY!)
- WISH FULFILLMENT (SHORT STORY)

Gus and Ghost Short Story Series:

- SEVENTH
- SEVENTH: FIRST FRUITS
- DEATH OF AN ALCHEMIST (UNCOLLECTED ANTHOLOGY)
- SEVENTH: THE SAMHAIN DILEMMA
- DARK OF THE MOON (UNCOLLECTED ANTHOLOGY)
- FLIGHT PLAN (UNCOLLECTED ANTHOLOGY)
- MIDSUMMER NIGHT (UNCOLLECTED ANTHOLOGY)

Logans of Lastalrig Series:

- HER HIGHLAND LAIRD (NOVELLA)
- HER HIGHLAND YULE (SHORT STORY)
- WISE WOMAN (SHORT STORY)

Red's Series:

- RED'S MAGICK (SHORT STORY COLLECTION)
- SEEING RED (SHORT STORY)

Signs of the Prophecy Novels:

- YOUNGEST
- SEEKER
- CHOSEN (COMING SOON!)

Sorcha's Children Series:

- SORCHA'S CHILDREN (OMNIBUS EDITION)
- SORCHA'S HEART (NOVELLA)
- DRAGONS' CHOICE (NOVEL)
- DRAGONS' FLIGHT (NOVEL)
- DRAGONS' DESIRE (NOVEL)
- DRAGONS' DESTINY (NOVEL)

Supernatural Yellowstone Short Story Series:

- REALITY BITES
- THE CAT LADY OF YELLOWSTONE

Uncollected Anthology Short Stories:

- DEATH OF AN ALCHEMIST (UA ALCHEMY)
- THE WEDDING CAKE (UA MAGICAL ARTS)
- DARK OF THE MOON (UA PARANORMAL PIRATES)
- IN THE BANYAN COPSE (UA UNEXPECTED HISTORIES)
- OLD ONE (UA MAGICAL QUESTS)
- HAVE HOARD, WILL SEEK (UA A DIVERSITY OF DRAGONS)
- FLIGHT PLAN (UA MYSTICAL MAPS)
- DISAPPEARED! (UA WERE-CREATURES & CONUNDRUMS)
- MIDSUMMER NIGHT (UA SUMMER SOLSTICE)

Universal Star League Short Story Series:

- Voyages Into The Black (Collection)
- The Warbirds of Absaroka
- Awakening the Warrior
- Incident on the Odyssey
- The Queen's Captive
- The Lost Colony
- Freighter Families in Space

Witchling Short Story Series:

- Witchling
- The Solitary Sorceress
- To Protect a Princess

Stand Alone Novels:

- Second Sight

Historical Fiction:

- Her Highland Laird (Novella)
- Her Highland Yule
- Incident on the High Line
- Miss Bainbridge's Summer Adventure
- Miss Bainbridge's Christmas Party
- Sisters in Suffrage
- The Trail Where We Cried
- The White Dragon and the Red

Short Story Collections:

- Love in a Flash
- Tales of Bygone Days
- Tales of Love & Magick
- Tales of the Unexpected
- Tales of Tomorrow
- Tales of Disastrous Deeds

Short Fiction:

- A Grove of Mountain Ash
- A Walk with Georgia
- An Alien Adventure
- Astromancer
- Because of the Christmas Stroll
- Beneath and Beyond
- Deep Dreaming
- Delia's Decision
- Egg Thief
- Enchantment, Inc.
- God-Touched
- Ice Storm
- Incident on the High Line
- In Search of a Valentinian
- Izzie
- Jolly Well Done
- Keystrokes & Intuition
- Miss Bainbridge's Christmas Party
- Miss Bainbridge's Summer Adventure
- Needle-Green
- New Year
- Opening Her Eyes
- Remembrance
- Silver-Tipped Death
- Simon Says
- Sisters in Suffrage
- Skye Dreams
- Spinning
- The Tie That Binds
- The Trail Where We Cried
- The White Dragon and the Red
- To Dream of Flying
- Treasures
- Trial on the Trail
- Wakinyan's Valley

"WDM Presents" Anthologies:

- SPUN YARNS UNWOUND, VOL. 1
- SPUN YARNS UNWOUND: VOL. 2
- SPUN YARNS UNWOUND: VOL. 3
- SPUN YARNS UNWOUND: VOL. 4
- SPUN YARNS UNWOUND: VOL. 5
- TALES OF MYSTERY & MAYHEM
- 2016: A YEAR OF SHORT FICTION
- 2017: A YEAR OF SHORT FICTION
- WDM PRESENTS: SHORT FICTION FROM 2018
- WDM PRESENTS: SHORT FICTION FROM 2019
- WDM PRESENTS: SHORT FICTION FROM 2020
- WDM PRESENTS: SHORT FICTION FROM 2021

PREVIEW: SORCHA'S HEART

If you enjoyed this collection, you may want to read *Sorcha's Heart*, the foundation novella for my *Sorcha's Children* series. Here's a sample:

Sorcha knotted her fists so tightly her knuckles whitened. She glared at her mother across the rough oak worktable. "When are you going to acknowledge me as a fully capable wizard? I'm not an apprentice anymore. I don't need your permission to seek the Heart of Fire."

"Fine," Elspeth shot back, "but I'm warning you this is a mistake. The Heart of Fire is dangerous." The small, compact woman stretched to reach the braid of garlic hanging from the beam above her head, yanked a bulb loose and tossed it to her daughter.

"So is this war!" Sorcha caught the bulb by reflex, slammed it on the table and separated out three cloves for the strengthening potion. Her gaze never left her mother. "Don't you realize how powerful dragons are? If Leofric continues on his present course, he'll push them too far. They'll wipe us off the face of the earth."

Fear flashed across Elspeth's face, and Sorcha knew that her mother agreed; the King's recent aggressive actions could have serious repercussions.

Sorcha's mood softened. She picked up her paring knife and began to chop the cloves, pondering the enigma of the woman who had given her not only life, but a heritage of magic. Because of that heritage, strangers often assumed they were sisters rather than mother and child. Elspeth's long, dark hair sported only an occasional strand of gray. Trim, active, healthy. These words described both her and her mother. Neither of them possessed the lush curves so desired by other women at court, but neither really noted the lack, being too concerned with the practice of magic to worry about attracting the opposite sex.

Elspeth's bright green eyes glowed with fervent belief and wily intelligence. Sorcha shared her mother's fervency and intelligence, but not her eyes. She had inherited her unknown father's eyes; deep blue, with an exotic slant that engendered frequent comparisons to cats' eyes.

"Yes. I do understand," Elspeth said with calm assurance, "and I'm trying to convince Leofric how dangerous his present policy is."

Sorcha opened her mouth to push home her advantage, but Elspeth held up a slim hand to stem the flow of words.

"But that doesn't mean I'm willing to sacrifice my only child."

She leaned forward, eyes wide, pleading and vulnerable. "Leave the Heart of Fire alone. It might end this war, but at what cost? Sorcha, you have no idea what that amulet will require as payment for its power."

A shiver ran down Sorcha's spine and she made a reflexive warding sign as she wiped her hands on the tattered hem of her potion-making apron.

Look for *Sorcha's Heart* at your favorite online retailer.

ABOUT DEBBIE MUMFORD

Debbie Mumford specializes in speculative fiction (fantasy, paranormal romance, and science fiction) as well as mystery and historical fiction. Author of the popular *Sorcha's Children* series, Debbie loves the unknown, whether it's the lure of space or earthbound mythology. Her work has been published in multiple volumes of *Fiction River*, as well as in *Heart's Kiss Magazine*, *Amazing Monster Tales*, and many other popular anthologies. She writes about dragon-shifters, time-traveling lovers, and detectives—whether amateur or professional—for adults as <u>Debbie Mumford</u>, and science fiction and fantasy for tweens and young adults as <u>Deb Logan</u>.

Join Debbie's special announcement newsletter list and receive a FREE story!

To learn more, visit Debbie at:
debbiemumford.com/
Or send her an email at:
deborah.mumford@gmail.com

f facebook.com/DebbieMumfordWrites
a amazon.com/author/debbiemumford
BB bookbub.com/authors/debbie-mumford
X x.com/deborah_mumford

www.ingramcontent.com/pod-product-compliance
Lightning Source LLC
Chambersburg PA
CBHW030352180626
46812CB00007B/2854